'Lewis Nordan's
WELCOME
TO THE
ARROW-CATCHER
FAIR

"Nordan wrote *Welcome to the Arrow-Catcher Fair* with a pen dipped in inky childhood memories. Characters that people the South hobble and dance across the pages of his short stories, each suffering from his own personal torment or delighting in his own black humor."
—United Press International

"Extraordinary... One is tempted to invoke the name of William Faulkner for the cadenced rhythms, and of Truman Capote or Carson McCullers for the gothic quality of the imagination that peoples [these] stories with a wondrous array of Southern grotesque. Add to it all a rollicking sense of humor, and you discover Lewis Nordan as an original, extraordinary writer."
—*Studies in Short Fiction*

"Nordan teases us with his own love of a good story, which we, like many of his inquisitive characters, are unable to resist."　　—*Publishers Weekly*

"An excellent example of the Southern Grotesque... well worth reading."　　—*Wall Street Journal*

ALSO BY Lewis Nordan,
AVAILABLE FROM VINTAGE CONTEMPORARIES

The All-Girl Football Team

WELCOME
TO THE
ARROW-CATCHER
FAIR

Vintage Contemporaries

VINTAGE BOOKS
A DIVISION OF RANDOM HOUSE, INC.
NEW YORK

WELCOME TO THE ARROW-CATCHER FAIR

Stories by
LEWIS NORDAN

First Vintage Contemporaries Edition, August 1989

Copyright © 1983 by Lewis Nordan

All rights reserved under International and Pan-American Copyright Conventions. Published in the United States by Random House, Inc., New York. Originally published, in hardcover, by Louisiana State University Press, Baton Rouge, Louisiana, in 1983.

Some of the stories in this volume originally appeared in *Harper's* and *Redbook*.

Library of Congress Cataloging-in-Publication Data
Nordan, Lewis.
    Welcome to the Arrow-Catcher Fair: stories / by
Lewis Nordan.
        p.   cm.—(Vintage contemporaries)
    Originally published: Baton Rouge: Louisiana State
University Press, 1983.
    ISBN 0-679-72164-9 : $6.95
    I. Title.
PS3564.O55W4   1989
813'.54—dc/19   88-40391
                                                              CIP

Manufactured in the United States of America
10   9   8   7   6   5   4   3   2   1

for Mary

CONTENTS

Mr. Nodine, Pentecost,
and the Oral Tradition / **3**

The Sin Eater / **21**

Rat Song / **35**

Wheelchair / **51**

Storyteller / **62**

The Copper Balloons / **71**

One-Man Band / **83**

Sugar Among the Freaks / **95**

Welcome to the Arrow-Catcher
Fair / **113**

WELCOME
TO THE
ARROW-CATCHER
FAIR

MR. NODINE,
PENTECOST, AND
THE ORAL TRADITION

Joe Moma Shirley opened the tube of massage cream and smeared Mr. Nodine's lips inside and out. He did not listen to the family legends of Moany, his grandmother, who stood at his back in the narrow tiled room. He was determined not to hear. The old tales enchanted and bewildered him, charmed him, but it was their charm that frightened him. He would not listen. And he tried also not to think of his wife's body, either of them, the regular, beautiful, sexy young body that he craved, or the other, the one she owned, the leathery, mummified old corpse that had stood in the broom closet for sixty-four years, the pencil peddler, Old Milt. He shut it all out except his work. Concentrating on closing Mr. Nodine's mouth, he passed the curved needle and thread in small perfect stitches through the inside of the lower lip and gums and up through the right nostril. The needle popped neatly through the nasal septum as he drew the thread back down to the upper lip and tied it off, closing the mouth as quickly and perfectly as he had ever done. He loved closing mouths. They would be shut forever. "You are so fine, Joe Moma, just like the other Shirleys, so strange and fine." Still he did not hear Moany.

Shirley Morocco, his wife, stood across from Joe Moma, staring into the reflection of fluorescent lights on ceramic tile, as if she were troubled. She was not an embalmer herself, but a fine assistant. Embalming fluid was in her veins, her grandfather used to tell her. But today something was surely wrong. It hurt Joe Moma to think that Old Milt might be distracting her, but he had to set his jaw, keep his mind on his work so he wouldn't hear Moany. He should never have agreed to let his grandmother live with them when Grandpa Shirley died in the quicksand, but it couldn't be helped now.

He set Mr. Nodine's jaw high enough to mold the same look of friendly defiance or firm compassion he had seen in the bank. It was a small thing; even Mrs. Nodine would probably never notice. It didn't matter.

Moany Shirley was saying, "Aunt Eva had not the slightest idea where he had gone." The words got through. Something about her voice made them penetrate.

"Who, Moany?" Joe Moma found himself saying, weakening, speaking softly so he would not yet have to admit to himself that he wanted to hear the story. He concentrated on not hearing the answer to his question, looking critically into Mr. Nodine's open bulging eyes, where he lay naked on the table. "Cotton pledgets," he said. Shirley Morocco tore the wrapper from a blue box and placed two pledgets, like coins, into his hand. Before she drew her hand away, she may have let it linger one second longer than necessary. It drove Joe Moma crazy with desire for her body, the regular one. He looked up but saw nothing in her green eyes except the mystery and yearning that were always there. Then he felt the forceps pass from her hand to his. He looked for one more second into her eyes. She drove him to the edge of insanity. He looked back into Mr. Nodine's bulging eyes, where meaning was not so elusive.

Moany Shirley said, "Grandpa Shirley's older brother, Sam." She seemed now to speak to no one but herself. Then it was hardest not to listen. "He walked six miles to the River bridge and jumped."

Joe Moma had never heard this one. He would listen just a little. No, no, he wouldn't. He would not listen. With the tiny forceps, he placed over each eyeball a small pad of disc-shaped cotton, first the left, then the right, more meticulous in his work than most men who are born into the art and not merely married into it. He would not listen to Moany.

"The very day Sam lost his wife," she continued. "On that day, he walked six miles to the River bridge and jumped." She chuckled a little, softly. The more disastrous the tale, the more it seemed to swell her fierce pride. She was proud, there was no denying it—but it was pride laced with a deadly irony, and it was hard not to listen.

Joe Moma shut it out as well as he could. Holding his breath, he closed each lid in its turn, careful not to overlap the uppers and lowers, careful to cover no more than two-thirds of the eyeball with the upper. When it was done, he released his breath slowly and smiled up at Shirley Morocco. She could not help smiling some, too. Proudly, he thought. But something, some quality of her smile, was depressingly tentative.

Moany's words got through again. "Lost his wife" was the phrase he heard. Something about it was wrong. Then he knew: "Moany," Joe Moma said, "that can't be true. Uncle Sam's wife didn't die until after Uncle Sam. She may not even be dead yet. I never knew Uncle Sam, but I met Aunt Eva several times. Sam was already dead." He had not wanted to speak, to concede that he was listening, interested, but he had to. It would not help, but he had to try. If he could prove just once that Moany was lying, making it all up, then maybe he could stop listening. Damnation, he thought, I shouldn't have got into this, but I think I've got her this time. Eva's not dead yet. He turned back to his work and tried not to listen.

"I never said Eva was dead. Of course not. She's one hundred and seven years old and raises rabbits in Benoit. Course she's not dead. I said Sam lost her." Now he was listening. "Lost her on the third of September in Belk-Hudsons department store at a white sale. 1954. Or thought he did. He was eighty-nine years old and as senile a man as you'd ever want to meet. Used to drink Dr. Tichenor's." Joe Moma stood above his work, waiting for the end, afraid he was losing Shirley Morocco but waiting anyway, statue-like, for the end of the story. "Eva said Sam walked around the store for a while—she got his part from the clerk—no more than ten minutes to hear Eva tell it, five maybe. He kept saying to himself, 'I seem to have lost my wife, I seem to have lost my wife.' You never hear Eva tell this?"

"No," Joe Moma whispered, abject, hopeless, trying to concentrate on Mr. Nodine, knowing that his resistance was already weak so doing no more than standing above his work with a few instruments in his hands, knowing also that he could not use them, could not even think of his wife and the corpse in her closet, which deep down he knew made her distant and cold today, not until he learned what happened to Great-uncle Sam, outraged at Moany for telling this but especially at himself for his weakness, his listening. "No, Moany, no," he said, whispered, because a whisper was the only voice that would come out, "tell it, tell what happened to Uncle Sam."

"You ought to hear Eva laugh when she tells this story." Moany was relaxed and comfortable. "She can tell it better than I can."

"Tell it, Moany, tell it," he said, or thought, he scarcely knew which, did not know whether his vocal chords were actually working. Sometimes they failed him. "Tell, Moany, tell." She had him now.

"Not much to it," she said, her voice comfortable and dreamy, the way it became when she knew she had all the time in the world. "Sam wandered around Belk's for a while saying, 'I seem to have lost my wife,' until what he was saying got stuck in his head." Moany was tickled now, trying to keep from laughing as she told the story. "Then he sort of came to himself, just for a minute, you know, like old folks'll do sometimes, Dr. Tichenor's or not." She stifled the hysterical laughter beneath the crusty surface of her voice. "Just sort of medium senile instead of all the way. Or would it be all the way instead of medium?"

Yes yes yes tell it Moany tell more tell it and be done. Where is the end? "Did he really jump?" Tell me all so I can be free.

Moany was laughing out loud now, more than chuckling, snorting. "Soon as he heard what he was saying, he walked the six miles to do just what he always said he would do if he lost Eva before he died himself." Yes yes yes he jumped didn't he, jumped into the Mississippi River and drowned? "Jumped off the bridge. Eva was bringing the Ford around at the time, the one she still has. Sam was supposed to stay in Belk's in the air conditioning." Joe Moma's head was reeling, but he recovered his voice and part of his mind. Leave it alone, his rational mind told him. Don't say more, it will be a mistake. But he was in too deep already. She would find a way to defeat him, to make the story still more outrageous and at the same time more believable, or at least irrefutable, but he could not keep from speaking.

"Moany," he said, "I don't believe a word of that."

"Believe it or not."

"Well, I don't."

"Don't what?"

"Believe it, Moany," he said. "I don't believe it."

"Ripley's."

"What? What do you mean?"

"Ripley's Believe It Or Not. 1964. Ten years after he jumped. I saw it in the Greenwood *Commonwealth*. Your Great-uncle Sam appeared in Ripley's Believe It Or Not for jumping off the Mississippi River bridge at Greenville." Joe Moma looked up at Shirley Morocco for support, but she seemed far away, tragic and lost and beautiful, as if she hid a dark secret and the secret made her more beautiful. He loved her so much. He turned back to Mr. Nodine and gently, thoughtfully massaged his eyes with cream.

He said, "It just isn't true. Even if Uncle Sam was crazy, senile, whatever you call it—even if he did jump off the River bridge— Ripley's wouldn't bother with it. Not a simple suicide. A drowning. That doesn't make him special, Moany. It makes him ordinary. The Shirleys are not weird, not extraordinary. They are mostly like me." He tried not to think of his grandfather, Council Mancil Fear God Shirley, who drove his motorcycle into the quicksand, or his own quiet, dear father, who sat this moment at home watching TV documentaries on the hibernation of bears on a television set that had not worked since 1971. "They are decent, normal people with normal jobs. Decent people, Moany, not strange or doomed, or not *especially* doomed, not celebrated for their doom. Ripley's didn't carry a drowning." He hated these disagreements. They drew him away from his wife, and he never won anyway. For the moment this one seemed to have fallen in his favor, but he knew it wasn't over.

"He didn't drown," Moany Shirley said. Joe Moma looked back at her, into the wildly powdered criss-cross of wrinkles in her face. "The River was low that year. Drought year." Joe Moma turned and straightened Mr. Nodine's arms and legs and raised his head onto a headrest so he seemed to look at his own feet. Work—pure concentration. It was the only thing that would keep Joe Moma from listening.

"1954. Summer of that year. Early fall really. Right after Labor Day." Joe Moma checked Mr. Nodine's neck for wrinkling. There was none. Good.

"The river was way down. Sam jumped through the top of a brand new 1954 Wayfarer Dodge with a man and woman from Indianola in the backseat." I knew it, Joe Moma thought, I knew it. "They'd parked down on the mud-flats. The ferryboat captain claims he heard Sam hit the car clear downstream, like a gong." She was chuckling and clucking and snorting with low appreciative laughter, sucking her teeth and holding back. Finally it all burst out, the laughter. She hooted and howled with gaiety. Tears flowed from her eyes. She told, as well as she could, between hysterical gasps, that the man and woman were taken directly to the insane asylum at Whitfield, where they spent the rest of their lives. At last she gained control of herself and immediately began another tale, one Joe Moma had already heard, the one about Heidi Shirley driving into Jackson with a dead buzzard on top of the car and what the buzzard held in its beak. He would be able to block this one out better than the last. It was easier when he had already heard the story. He had trained himself.

Though he sensed that Shirley Morocco wanted to speak, he could not listen to her either. Not because he did not want to listen, he wanted that more than anything, but because if he did, he

would also hear the legends of Moany. They would make him become a man he did not want to be, his own mind, like hers,
mummified in the past. He wanted to live for today, for his wife
and his work, not for the old tales. But the tales fascinated him
horribly, drew him in, and imprisoned his mind. He had trained
himself not to listen, but it was a constant, awful process, like lipreading to a deaf person. Hoping, not desperately but only abjectly, resignedly, that what Shirley Morocco was saying could
wait, he pushed all thought aside and plunged back into his work.
Extending Mr. Nodine's left arm palm up, he made a quick, precise incision exactly two inches long, just below the edge of the
armpit. "Forceps," he said, and felt a coolness snap into his hand.
He looked up. Moany was talking, but he did not hear. He had
his concentration back.

Seeing Shirley Morocco standing so beautifully and solemnly
countenanced, across the embalming table, made him think of two
days ago when she cried, when he asked whether they might bury
Old Milt. Unable to bear her tears, he took her in his arms and
said, "Keep him then, keep Old Milt forever, as long as he lasts, if
that will make you happy." He held her close. "But"—here he
was careful, gentle—"but, Shirley Morocco, be discreet. Don't
show him off to everybody who comes around. I need that
promise."

"Why should you be ashamed of him?" she sobbed. "The
Shirleys have just as many skeletons in their closet as any family
in this town, not that Old Milt is a skeleton, so please don't play
high and mighty with me." Joe Moma could not bring himself
to parse this problem, it was too much for him. "Is it because you
think he was a beggar?" Her voice was cruel.

"Shirley Morocco . . ."

"You think because a man dies and nobody ever claims him
that makes you better?" Her eyes were emerald fire. "Well, then,
you know nothing, Joe Moma Shirley. Thousands of people love
Old Milt. They have come to this mortuary by the thousands over
the last three generations—since August 23, 1911, to be exact—
and do you know why?" The question needed no answer. "Be-

cause they love him." She was defiant now, bold and proud. "Pa Zippy, my own grandfather, who embalmed Old Milt—and did a very fine job, I might add—he said there was gold-work in his teeth ten times better than anything that could have been done in America at that time. Does that sound like a common beggar? Does it?"

"I know that, Shirley Morocco," he said, trying to calm her. "And even if he didn't have the gold-work, it wouldn't matter to me. It simply doesn't matter. And I know he wasn't a beggar. He was a pencil peddler. Outside a tent revival. It was an honorable death, and he should be buried, like other dead people. It's in the natural order of things, Shirley Morocco—a man lives, he dies, is embalmed, and buried. It's as simple as that."

"Don't get sarcastic with me, Joe Moma Shirley."

"If . . ."

"Maybe some other people I know would be better off if they had more spiritual feelings themselves and didn't worry so much about getting people into the ground before their time." Her voice was a virtual chant now, a liturgy learned long ago: "The mortician is a tool of the final Resurrection. Those are Pa Zippy's own words, Joe Moma. If you can't believe that, then we have nothing more to talk about."

The memory was unpleasant. "The smaller ones," he said, patient. He handed the forceps back to Shirley Morocco.

"Sorry," she said. She corrected her mistake and gave Joe Moma the five inchers. He wanted to hold her, to say something, to say, "Shirley Morocco, I love you so much, nothing matters except you."

He said nothing. When the small forceps came into his hand, he pushed all thoughts of her aside and, with the instrument, skillfully dissected the fatty and fibrous tissue beneath the skin, using swift, deft strokes parallel to the vessels so as not to injure them.

"Joe Moma," he suddenly heard his wife say. Why now? Joe Moma wanted to complain, why talk now? Why not before he had started the dissection, before his grandmother started a new story? He did not want to listen to Shirley Morocco, because if he did he would also hear Moany and feel the loneliness that goes with family pride, the lostness that he felt when he admitted he was not one man doing something new and singular and individual but a tentative product of a great amalgam of men and women in a long, strange, continuous line stretching out to infinity until he too became not Joe Moma the embalmer who made a trade an art, but a legend of Joe Moma Shirley, one more eccentric in a great mythic succession of loonies marching in lockstep toward disaster. And yet he could not send Moany away, either, not after his solemn promises at the quicksand pit that she could always live with him, always watch each embalming, just as she had watched Fear God Shirley's before she sold the ruined motorcycle, and that when she needed to talk he would always listen. He had not known that her mind would snap like an icicle in a perpetual witch's winter and that she would talk incessantly during every waking hour of every day after that singular day on which the motorcycle left the Petticocowa bridge and landed squarely on top of Fear God in the quicksand and pushed him peacefully as a pig under the strange, blond dirt while rattling motorcycle, in a haze of blueish smoke, sank slowly, majestically above him for perhaps fifteen minutes, the headlight beaming skyward, the front wheel becoming invisible last of all, like a sinking ship on deep calm seas. Oh, Lord, Lord, he thought, I've got to keep my mind on my work, the first moments of entry. Maybe I can work and sort of listen at the same time. At that moment, the axillary artery and vein came into view. They were beautiful. He could not answer Shirley Morocco, he would not listen to Moany. With the forceps, Joe Moma probed on. The axillaries virtually hypnotized him each time he exposed a set. Moany talked, but he did not hear.

"Joe Moma," Shirley Morocco said again, louder, intent that he hear, but also apologetic and humble. "I've—I've done something terrible to you." Oh, Shirley Morocco, darling, not now, he thought, please not now. The axillary vein was prominent and distended, magnificent yet delicate and pure as any structure in a corpse, its translucent walls as blue as a headstone of pure lapis lazuli. Mr. Nodine had a beautiful set of axillaries. The artery was directly behind the vein, hiding, perfectly white, like the multitude of nerves in which it seemed to crouch, timid as a white bunny in a snowbank. "Aha," Joe Moma said, whispered, "so there you are." He was excited and sweating. The arteries had none of the longitudinal streaking of the nerves—that's what gave this one away—and when he rolled it between his thumb and forefinger, he felt it collapse. It was the axillary all right, and my God, it felt good.

"So he was cross-eyed for the rest of his life," a voice said. Joe Moma looked up. Somewhere he had lost track. Somewhere between the beginnings of Shirley Morocco's confession, which vaguely came back to him now, and the discovery of the axillary, Moany Shirley's disasters had wormed their way back into his consciousness. He could not keep up with all of it. "Cross-eyed for the rest of his natural life, and divorced on top of that." Shirley Morocco handed him a small scalpel and a few pieces of thin nylon twine already cut. His concentration was broken; he had to try to get it back.

"I know this is not a perfect time to tell you this, Joe Moma," Shirley Morocco seemed to be saying, "but . . . "

"Cross-eyed?" he heard himself say.

"Yes, oh yes," Moany Shirley said, perversely, perhaps ironically, "Cousin Hugh—actually your third cousin . . . "

Joe Moma forced his mind back to Mr. Nodine's axillary. When a two-inch segment of vein showed clearly, he milked the blood toward the heart with his fingers and clamped the vein shut with the blunt-nosed artery forceps. It felt good. Around the vein and about an inch apart, he placed two ligatures and tied the lower one tightly. "Scissors," he said. He cut the vein halfway through, neat as a surgeon. The perfect reconciliation of art and science, he thought. "Vein tube." Shirley Morocco had it ready.

"He sat on his own scrotum."

Get out of my mind, disasters, Joe Moma thought, pushing the vein tube and rubber drain attachment into the vein. He felt with his thumb to be certain the plunger was all the way in. "Is the drain-tank ready, Shirley Morocco?"

She checked the tank. "Yes."

Joe Moma raised Mr. Nodine's elbow a little to let the tube bypass the blockage near the collarbone and shoved the instrument steadily through the superior vena cava. He hoped it would reach the right atrium.

"I don't know why I didn't tell you in the beginning," Shirley Morocco said. "It was a petty thing on my part. I can admit that now. But two days ago . . . " Her voice passed out of hearing.

It was almost there. Please let it reach the atrium.

"But now it's too late to stop them."

He felt the drain tube slip in. Joe Moma was pleased. Very little blood to sop up with cotton. He tied off the other segment of vein with thread so the tube held steady.

"It crushed his right testicle and left him with his eyes permanently crossed." It was Moany.

Immediately, he went to work on the artery—cutting, inserting the tube, clamping. Not much blood here either. He worked steadfastly, desperately trying not to listen to Moany Shirley, yet trying to hear without listening, trying to hear Shirley Morocco at the same time. What was she trying to confess?

"I received the phone call two days ago," Shirley Morocco said, "just after our—you know—argument." He was not looking at her, but he felt her eyes turn away, maybe down toward the floor, maybe toward the broom closet in the next room. Argument—?

Joe Moma lifted the gallon jug of Royal Bond to the table and filled the large syringe. It was an old-fashioned method—he knew that. He could have used the pumps; the Zippy Morocco Mortuary had all the latest equipment. But this was safer, and more artistic, he believed.

"So they're coming this afternoon," one voice said.

Oh yes, he thought, yes, of course, the argument. Old Milt. His chest tightened with a momentary panic, but he suppressed the feeling. He wished they could talk about this some other time.

"Completely ruined him for his chosen profession for the remainder of his life," said the other voice. Once he let one in, the other could always wheedle its way in, too.

Joe Moma squeezed off first one bulbful, then two, then a third, in the direction of the hand, slowly but with firm pressure. The veins in Mr. Nodine's hand and forearm stood out prominently as the arm began to firm up. The fluid was circulating. Good, good, couldn't ask for better.

"Cousin Hugh was a crowd estimator for the Treasury Department until this happened, until he sat on his testicles and crossed his eyes. It was a good job, too."

Joe Moma stroked the arm from the hand upwards, milking the fluid back into the body. He stopped occasionally to inject more, and watched the muscles increase in bulk and become firmer as the solution reached them, like a weight-lifter's.

"Joe Moma," Shirley Morocco said, "do you hear me? They are coming this afternoon. In a few minutes, probably. The children from Marietta, Georgia."

"But when Hugh got both his eyes crossed, the government thought he better just try to find different work. Thought he couldn't handle crowd-estimating any more. You know—plus his right testicle taking so long to get over the soreness."

Mr. Nodine's cheeks were full as a baby's and the eyeballs beneath the closed lids stood up hard and firm.

"There will be a busload of them, the children. They're part of a Pentecostal Holiness retreat."

" . . . do the job as well as ever. Just divide all his estimates by two."

A full gallon was in Mr. Nodine's circulatory system now, and still not a hitch, not one flaw. Joe Moma was sweating profusely now, hot and excited. His hands trembling and his hair wet, Joe Moma pumped on.

"Do you understand me, Joe Moma?" Shirley Morocco's voice

was impatient for the first time. Her impatience broke through his fevered consciousness just as he pulled the plunger out of the vein tube and a thick glob of undiluted blood shot out into the glass jar beneath it.

"He tried to get a full disability pension . . . "

The thinner blood-and-formalin solution drained rapidly behind the first thick globs and steadily filled the jar.

"This is their first big rest stop of the trip," Shirley Morocco said. "I did just what I knew Daddy and Pa Zippy would have done . . . "

" . . . but he never could bring himself to fill out the Social Security forms saying how he got them crossed."

"I invited them to come through the mortuary to see Old Milt."

Joe Moma was exhausted and breathing fiercely. He didn't know if he could go on. Silently the jar at his feet continued to fill. Joe Moma raised his sweat-blurred eyes and looked up from the table at his wife. The confinement of the room increased. All that she had been trying to tell him suddenly coalesced in his mind. Now it made sense. Moany's tale began coming through and coalescing now as well, the two stories winding together like snakes on a staff.

"No," he said, but no word came out, no sound. "Oh, no." Still no words were coming, not even the sound of released air, but somehow, as though he were speaking underwater, the words seemed to form themselves plaintively in the air above him in the room. "Oh, no, not children, not now, not crossed testicles, not broken eyes . . . "

"They are on their way to Miracle Valley, Arizona."

"No." There was a little sound now, but not much.

"His wife left him, of course, on account of the busted ball. He had already ruined the other one, the left one, when he was in high school, so after he sat on the right one, they were both gone. No way to get one back once it's gone."

Mr. Nodine drained on, the stream from the vein tube gradually running more slowly.

"No, Shirley Morocco, Moany, it isn't possible." He was actually speaking now, his larynx was working again, but only softly, and he was not entirely sure which woman he aimed his protests at. "No, it just can't be."

"The county school over in Bolivar County, back before they ever consolidated." Who had said that? He tried to get a grip on his mind.

Finally, he said, "You can't let them do it, Shirley Morocco, you can't let them."

"Lost it in the track and field events."

"We have to, Joe Moma," Shirley Morocco said. "It's for a lesson on the Resurrection. Besides, there's no way to stop them."

"Hugh didn't wear his athletic supporter that day."

"They're on the way. I'm sorry. It's all I can say. And I can't turn them away from our door, after they've come so far."

" . . . and the high hurdles had a strand of barbed wire stretched across the top . . . "

Joe Moma was distressed by the news of the Pentecostal children, so distressed that he missed hearing why there was barbed wire on the hurdles. He had to get his mind together. He still had Mr. Nodine's body cavity ahead of him. When the drainage had stopped completely Joe Moma sutured the incision and massaged the area with cream. Work fast, he told himself, the children are coming and you are losing Shirley Morocco.

Moany had started another story. "You never knew Lolly St. Vincent Shirley, did you? No, couldn't have," she said.

He heard but did not answer. Another problem had come up. When he pushed Mr. Nodine's arm to his side, it would not stay there. It rose slowly outward, as though he were pointing to the door behind Joe Moma. Ah, God, Joe Moma thought, ah, God. I should have used the carotids instead. Oh, goddamn.

"She married into the family through Otis Shirley, the sheriff down in Scott County."

Mr. Nodine's arm would not stay down. It would not. The formalin had stiffened it into what might have been a permanent left-turn signal. Joe Moma felt panicky. There was not much he could do. "If they come before we finish," he said, "you mustn't, you—please don't go out there. Don't leave me for him. Please don't."

"I'll have to," she said, "you know that." He knew. "They want to see Old Milt. I can't refuse them."

"Look, darling," he said, "I'm going to use the trocar next, the aspirator." He held up the metal tube for her to see. "Help me, stay with me."

"Joe Moma," she said, "don't do this."

He inserted it into the slit in Mr. Nodine's upper pelvis and filled the room with its slurping. "Stay with me."

"I can't make a rash promise, Joe Moma. Please don't ask me again."

He lay the trocar aside and turned back to Mr. Nodine's stiffened arm. He pushed at it. It was no use. Each time he released it, the arm rose slowly out and pointed to the door.

"Tragic thing," a voice said. "Killed in World War II. Iwo Jima." The words got through. It was Moany Shirley's distant, dreamy voice again, the mystical but crazily ironic voice in which Joe Moma suspected she must make up these tales. Though he did not yet look back at her, the sound of her voice told him she had focused on something in the middle distance, or beyond—she had taken the classic pose for inventing legends of family disaster. She was making it all up, every word—he believed that with all his heart. She was crazy, not just eccentric, she was totally insane, as insane as he had been to make a promise more difficult to keep than any promise in the world, as insane as he was to keep an insane promise to an insane woman when his wife would not even promise to bury a corpse that had remained unburied for sixty-four years as though it were a dinosaur in a museum and, even more insanely, would not promise to keep from exhibiting it to a busload of Pentecostally Insane Holiness children, themselves perhaps especially resurrected from the crowd of whooping children who must have played outside the tent or sat with their parents in the revival meeting on a sultry night in August of 1911 when a man died leaning against a tree clutching a handful of pencils and carrying a pocketful of nickels, selling his wares, and hearing as he died an insane Pentecostal preacher's voice battering all of their brains with a fable of Death personified as an insane man galloping a blind white horse whose sides did not bleed when he dug them with silver spurs because Christ Is Risen Christ Is Risen Christ Is Risen Indeed. She was making it all up, every word— her voice told him so. But this voice also made him believe the tales, believe they were absolute and gospel truth, as true as the sock-footed corpse who this very moment stood in the broom closet, in 1911 a living, breathing, groveling, lonely, hungry white man and now in 1975 a moustached bespectacled Ken doll the color of walnut and stiff as a five-foot-four-inch oaken two-by-four, peering from behind the mops through eyes painted on the closed lids in 1948 by some other embalmer, a cousin-in-law, Ballew Alonzo Morocco, who painted eyes and attired the corpse doll at the expense of the Morocco family in a black suit with a gold watch chain, dressed him (save his shoes) in readiness for, perhaps, the broom closet prom to which he will escort some Barbie or Shirley or other doll-like woman who will love him for no other reason than that he is hers, her family's, a tradition but as though he could love her as well, lie beside her in darkness and breathe her sweet cow-breath when she sleeps and bring her flesh alive with his own, though his internal organs collapsed long ago and his external one became part of his mummified leg before Shirley Morocco was even born. Joe Moma believed and he didn't believe. They were the same.

"I hear the bus." It was Shirley Morocco's voice. Bus! He must not faint, he must get hold of himself. The Pentecostal children were here. His mind darted back to Mr. Nodine. He could tie the arm down, maybe. What an awful concession, though; what a complete loss of subtlety. There is not one iota of irony in a corpse whose arm must be tied down.

On the instant he heard the airbrakes of the bus, he also understood what in Moany Shirley's story had grabbed his attention. Otis Shirley could not have been killed in World War II and still be sheriff of Scott County, or any county in Mississippi, for

that matter. Or the world. And Otis was still sheriff. Joe Moma
had met him only recently. He remembered now. Perfect health.
What did it mean? He looked up for help, frantic, but found none.
Shirley Morocco was not across the table from him; she had already gone into the next room to guide the Pentecostal tour past
the broom closet, to carry on the Morocco tradition. Moany Shirley talked on and on. It was not Otis who was killed in the war,
she said, it was Aunt Lolly, his wife. Lolly St. Vincent Shirley was
killed on Iwo Jima on February 20, 1945, just one day after the
landing.

"Oh, my God!" Joe Moma screamed, the vocal chords letting
some sound through, as Mr. Nodine's arm crept back out again.
"I can't stand it, I can't listen to any more." But he had to listen;
he had to try—or try not—which was it? They were the same.
The children in the next room were laughing and shrieking now.
"His eyes, his eyes!" one of them shouted, in joy. "Look at Old
Will's eyes!"

"Old Milt, not Old Will," he heard his wife correct the child.
The others cheered and shouted that his right leg was shorter than
the left, that a hand was withered. "Hooray, hooray, hooray!"
they cheered. "Get in line, children, get in line, so everybody will
have a chance to see," a pastoral voice chided, a man's voice, the
minister's, Joe Moma supposed. "This is your tour guide, Mrs.
Shirley Shirley." Joe Moma could only squeal and splutter with
nervous rage, but no one could hear him. He wanted to scream,
"Not Shirley Shirley—nobody has that accursed name, not twice,
not double-damned! Shirley Morocco; tell them, tell them it's not
Shirley Shirley!" But before the squeals could turn into words,
he heard Shirley Morocco above the children's voices. She said,
"Old Milt was a legend in his own time," and Joe Moma began
squealing and squalling and grunting in a different key, trying to
say, "He was not! He was a pathetic bum in his own time! A goddamn pencil-peddler! He's a legend in *my* time, *on* my time, *yours*.
We don't even know his real name!" But before those words could
come out, he suddenly realized he had missed the end of Moany's
war story. Oh, God, oh my God, help me. Another tale had al-

ready begun. He mopped his sweaty arm across his face and spun around, violently, to look at her, to look wildly into Moany's own wild eyes. "How!" he screamed. It was not a question but a demand, and his voice was full of both rage and outrage. "How! How did it happen!" Froths of spittle flew from his mouth and collected at the corners. "How did his wife get killed on Iwo Jima! Tell me now! I can't take it. How did she do it? There were no women on Iwo Jima. Tell me now! And why in God's name was there a strand of barbed wire on the high hurdles? I want to know!"

"Everyone will have a chance to see, just stay in line." The pastoral and wifely voices were almost simultaneous in their admonition, their coaxing. He heard the minister and Shirley Morocco laugh confidentially at the coincidence of their voices.

Moany Shirley seemed to hear none of it, talking on. "Yes, oh Lord, yes," she said, with her strange cheerfulness, laughing with vicious glee, "yes, it was awful. Aunt Rhema's toe broke off in her shoe and she never let on, got right on the train."

The voice from the other room said, "We believe from certain dental evidence that Old Milt comes from European nobility. We believe he is an Italian count."

"Goddamnit, goddamnit, goddamnit," Joe Moma said, over and over, through clenched teeth, turning back to his work, still goddamning as he turned, violently grabbing the trocar from the instrument table, all alone with his Moany and his goddamning, bending over Mr. Nodine and slipping the tube into the upper pelvis, goddamning them all as he finished what he had begun.

"We have no proof of his lineage, of course. It is our *belief*."

Moany Shirley was chuckling and snorting. "You are so fine and strange, Joe Moma, you certainly are."

THE SIN EATER

Later, when the child would go over these events in his mind, he would imagine the old woman, Mrs. Tremble, as she would have appeared a moment before she heard the sound of the ambulance. The peacocks, living wild in the cottonwoods, descendants of birds that once strutted tame across this property, would have heard the siren first. Their shrieks and shrill comedy might have alerted her, their thunderous bustle and flutter across pastures and into the deeper woods. The slave-built house, with its spacious porch and gently sagging roofline, visible from the child's bedroom if he had thought to look a hundred yards across the goat pasture, would have sat bright and unchanged in the late-morning sun. Inside the house would have sat Mrs. Tremble, by a small fire in her living room. Her high windows would be closed, as would the drapes, against the first chill of the Mississippi autumn. A floor lamp, with a brass base and a tasseled shade, would be her only light. When the sound of the siren reached her, she would remove her glasses from their place on her nose and lay aside the needlepoint motto on which she had been working. "What on earth can it be?" she might have said, in her ridiculous, grandmotherly way. "I swan." She would have put aside the pipe that she was smoking.

The child who would imagine her was ten years old, named

Robert McIntyre. In his bedroom, in this more modest house, he saw the green bottle, which he had filled with kerosene. He saw it touch the lips of his baby brother. Like a kiss, he thought, even as the oily fluid flowed over the lips and off the infant's chin. Even as the little head jolted backwards. The eyes rolled up and became white and senseless. The baby had drunk the kerosene Robert was hiding. The kerosene he had thought even a parent could not find.

But Robert did not move, not yet. He could not. His brother, already unconscious but not yet fallen, weaved drunkenly, like a comic actor on a television screen. Who was that actor, Robert thought. The child fell, and the bottle clattered against the floor. The kerosene darkened the wood, and Robert saw the future. He knew his brother would not live. As soon as he knew that, he screamed.

He lifted his brother's head. With his too-short fingers he reached into the narrow throat to call back the kerosene and cause the accident not to have happened. An oily froth covered Robert's fingers, warmly. The pupilless eyes were still open. Then, in revulsion, he jerked away. He stood above his brother and scrubbed his fingers against his pants.

He saw the objects of his house, and the sounds and persons, as if they were old, recognizable photographs. There was his mother on the telephone. There was the empty bottle, the stain on the floor. There was a voice, the color of indigo, his mother's voice, and there were his own words, like mice, scuttering and scurrying and contemptible. A white ambulance was in the driveway, surrounded by the peacock's cries, and, immediately, his father's car also. Robert noticed two patches of rust on the roof of the car and found that he hated his father for them.

His father's voice seemed to be the color of grapes. It said, "Robbie, listen. Go to Mrs. Tremble's. Tell Mrs. Tremble what happened. I'll call from the hospital." When his mother came back into the room, Robert realized he had been seeing her all these years only in miniature, as if he looked at a dense concentration of the woman and not, perhaps, as everyone else had already seen her. She seemed now to be a tree, one of the ancient sycamores in

the back pasture, silver-blue and enormous. A redtailed hawk
swooped near but did not light, balancing upon the wind.

When the ambulance was gone, Robert was alone. He stared
at the bottle, which was no longer there, because his father had
taken it in the ambulance, but which he could still see. The bottle
he had filled and hid. The kerosene he planned to use for—he
didn't know what. Games, on the lakebank. Little fires.

Before the sound of the words reached him, or any sound, he
knew Mrs. Tremble was in the room. Kindly fat rich ancient
shaky-hands old Mrs. Tremble, with the white hair and wild peacocks and the gaseous aroma of pipe tobacco and face powder.
Her breath preceded her like a messenger of lightning and thunder.
"Robert," said her voice. "What on earth has happened, child? I
saw the ambulance." Robert turned to face her, since doing so was
unavoidable. Because of her concern, perhaps, she had become
even more of what she had always been, old and quiet and kind
and repulsive and grandmotherly, and somehow frightening now
as well. She had thin, pale lips, which seemed always to be
chapped. In them were tiny vertical lines that looked painful, and
her breath, which could travel long distances without diminution
of effect, stank like a pipe-smoker's. Though she was never actually known to smoke a pipe, it was never doubted by any child
who drew within her considerable range that she did so and that
the pipe, should it ever be discovered, would be of briar and grotesque of shape and deadly poison. "Whatever in the world has
happened, child?"

In Mrs. Tremble's living room, Robert became very small. By
magic, he had shrunk, as soon as he walked through the front
door. He sat as far forward as possible in a blue brocaded chair,
but still his feet would not touch the floor. His elbows, no matter
how hard he strained, would not rest comfortably on the chair
arms. He had been in this room many times, but it had never
shrunk him before. The colors had never been so bright, nor the
ceilings so high. Long-necked golden birds shrieked at him from
the Chinese carpets. There was a tiny fire in the fireplace, though
it was only October and not really cold yet, and there was a

smell, sulfurous and sickening, which Robert believed must be
the moist, solid residue of Mrs. Tremble's breath, growing and
reproducing in the rugs and drapes and upholstered chairs.

Mrs. Tremble fussed around the room, out again and back
again, monstrously cheerful. Everything would be fine, she said,
just fine. Her breath streaked around the room like a laser,
rebounding from the walls and floors and ceiling. Robert watched
it and stayed out of its path. What Robert must do, she said, must
promise her right this minute he would do, was not worry. Worry
was by far the worst thing in the world he could do right now.
His little brother was going to be fine, yes siree, just you wait and
see. Robert was afraid she might hug him, but she stayed her distance. Her breath idled between them like an engine.

There was to be a choice: Lemonade, or hot chocolate, or
spiced tea. Now which would it be? she wanted to know. Which
do you choose? He could have a cinnamon stick with the tea, she
promised. For a moment a strange feeling passed through his
body. He believed he might be a character in a book that somebody
else was reading. He looked at Mrs. Tremble, and at her breath.
It was the spiced tea that made him wonder. He tried to see Mrs.
Tremble as he had seen his mother, the larger tree in which her
miniature was contained. But nothing changed. He could see
nothing differently. "No, thank you, Mrs. Tremble," he said.
"Nothing for me, thanks."

So he waited. He moved from the brocaded chair to the fire
and looked into the little wreckage of coals. Even the fire had an
odd smell, a little too sweet, as if she might be burning
applewood. The firescreen was black and large, with tiny brass
handles at either side. The poker and shovel and tongs were also
heavy and black. When he tried to think of his brother's dying, he
found that he could not. He remembered Jack and the Beanstalk,
disobedient child of a grieving mother. The harp and hen and
golden eggs. The race downward through vegetation, the ax, the
collapse and fall and death of the giant. The green breath streaked
suddenly over his right shoulder and made the fire blaze up.

Sparks crackled and shot up the chimney. "Do you like the fire, Robert?" said the words that came trailing in the wake.

He struggled not to flinch. He thought of Hansel in the wooden cage. He saw Gretel stare deep into the oven. He braced himself but could not force himself to turn and meet her unbelievable, cheery eyes, or risk breathing her fumes. "Yes m'am," he said, into the fire. Did he like the fire? What might such a question mean? "Yes, it's nice," he said. "A nice little fire."

There had been a grass fire once, set accidentally by his father in the back pasture. Robert helped fight it with rakes and wet rugs. The smoke burned his chest when he breathed it, but Robert had not minded. When it spread to the edge of the woods, tractors plowed lanes around the flames. His father, riding one of the tractors, was the handsomest man in the world that day. His eyes had streamed with tears in the smoke. There was a gasoline fire too, another day, set by a child Robert's age. It caught the child's clothes and burned his jeans and boots into the flesh. Robert had not seen it; only, later, the grafted skin. He had seen it in his dreams, though. He had smelled the flesh and rubber in his dreams. There was a house too that burned, a shack. He remembered the pathetic few pieces of furniture someone had saved. They sat beside the smoking ashes and standing chimney, a chair, a wooden table, a dark wardrobe. They sat in the weather, long after the ashes had cooled and washed away. They whitened and rotted and finally were gone. There would have been his own little fires, on the lakebank. The kerosene. Burning ships, forts surrounded by Indians, volcanoes, human sacrifice. He wondered if kerosene felt like fire in the baby's throat. He wondered how people died.

Once, in a museum, he had thought of dying. He saw a stiff brown hunk of contorted clay in a glass case, and he learned it was a mummified child. This was the first time he ever thought he might die. He had seen his father kill wild dogs, the packs that sometimes came out of the woods and took down a goat, or larger stock. Brass shell casings would leap from the rifle, and the animals would scatter and drop. Sometimes they were only wounded, and his father would close their clear eyes at closer range.

He went outside the house. A noisy, noxious rocket of pipe-smoker's breath streaked past his ear and struck a fencepost deep in the pasture. It crumbled and collapsed into ashes, and the six-gauge barbed wire fell slack in that section. The voice said, "Robert. Oh, Robert dear. Won't you need a coat, child?" Beds of fireants crackled and burned and lay silent and gray and motionless. "Please don't go far. Promise you won't, Robert. If anything happened to you, I'd . . . " What would she do? he thought. Would she die? He tried not to wish that she would die. He tried not to wish that he would die. "I'm sorry," he prayed.

He was deep in the back pasture now. A she-goat was stuck by her horns, like small scimitars, in the squares of fence wire, where she had tried to reach a sweeter clump of grass. He walked to the crying animal and released the horns. He crossed the fence and walked toward the lake and woods.

It was afternoon now, and the air had more chill than he had thought. He could not go back for his jacket. What kind of person would call a boy "Robert dear" or "child"? What kind of person would have pipesmoker's breath and shaky hands and be named Mrs. Tremble?

The trees had begun some subtle change. The black-green lushness of September had become a lighter, friendlier green. The persimmons were ripe on the trees, and sullen wasps staggered fat and gorged in the pink-gold sweetness of the fallen fruit. Here and there he noticed hardwoods in which some of the leaves were already brown, but most were still green and, every so often, in a spreading oak or maple, a bouquet of red and yellow leaves appeared like decorations. The squirrels were busy; acorns were thick underfoot.

To his left, from a thicker brake of trees and cane, emerged first the movement and then the head and then the entirety of a large dog. A fear rippled through him and caused him to forget the afternoon chill. He did as his father had taught him. He kept an

eye on the wild dog and, at the same time, scanned the woods to
see whether there was a pack. He started a slow movement backwards, trying to put distance, a tree or two, if possible a fence,
between them. He kept looking. He could not find a pack, not
another dog, no movement in the woods or cane. The dog before
him was long-legged and black and thin. The long muscles
seemed almost to show through the matted hair.

He backed away. The dog had not yet really looked at him,
not directly. It sniffed the ground and raised its chin to the breeze.
It did not look, but it was aware of him. Robert looked hard at
the dog and thought he saw something, something like himself
and other than himself. He was distracted by a noise that, at first,
he thought belonged to the wind.

"Robert, oh Robert dear." Pipesmoker's breath blazed through
the trees and pasture, killing leaves and grass, setting fire to old
birdnests. The surface of the lake was choppy and uneven. The
wind increased and raised chillbumps on his bare arms. He remembered the years he had been the only child in his family. He
remembered the fear and the envy he felt when his father came to
his room. "Robbie," he had said, "son. You're going to be a big
brother. Can you believe it? Mama's going to have a baby." He
remembered the loathing. He looked at the two of them, mother
and father, and imagined the cloying sexuality, vague and terrible,
the dominance of his father upon his mother's nakedness. "It's the
gift of life," his father had said. Afterwards, Robert held the child
and began to love it. He gave him its bottle and was thankful his
mother had not breast-fed. He brought friends home from school
and showed them the baby. He taught them to hold its head. He
learned to forget the baby and, in that way, to love it more. He
went to fourth grade and learned to play two songs on a plastic
recorder; he kissed Melissa Townley outside the skating rink. He
helped his father bale alfalfa for the goats; he took pictures with
his father's reflex camera and learned to read a light meter. "Oh,
Robert dear. Telephone."

He turned from the dog and walked through the pasture, deliberately not running, but walking fast and, twice, almost falling. He looked back. The dog had lain down and was licking a paw. The goats bleated and fanned away. "Here I am, Mrs. Tremble," he said. "I'm coming."

The telephone was on the wall, a boxy, old-fashioned instrument that only Mrs. Tremble would have owned. The earpiece was shaped like a bell and was separate from the mouthpiece, which was part of the wooden box.

His father had not meant to tell him on the phone, but Robert asked the question directly and made him answer. The answer was no surprise: the child, Robert's brother, was dead. Robert had known. All through himself, inside as well as outside, Robert felt a pain, like that that seemed so constant in Mrs. Tremble's split, chapped lips. Then the silence was over. "These will be lonely, bad days, son," the voice said, his father. It was impossible to imagine a voice so kind or so tired. "But it's no one's fault."

"I love you, Daddy."

"I love you."

"Tell Mama . . . "

When he had hung up, Robert remembered a movie he had seen on television, a western, filmed in Utah and full of wide desert and red buttes. A faint cold fear thrilled through him. He thought of graves and of museums with large bottles filled with fetuses, two-headed sheep and piglets with human faces. He felt responsible for each one. No warmth, he thought. No breath. He tried to pray for museums. He asked forgiveness for siamese twins and freak shows. No tears came to him, and he was dry all through.

A meteor of Mrs. Tremble's breath struck the gold-colored drapes on the west windows and exploded into light like the sun. "It will be better with them open," she might have said. She pulled the tasseled cord hanging beside the windows and made the light from the floor lamp unnecessary. Robert watched her carefully, knowing that she knew. But she did not try to hug him or kiss him. She moved slowly through the room and seemed older than ever. Robert didn't know what to do. "He's dead," he told her, having nothing else to say.

Without answering him, Mrs. Tremble moved to a table that sat in the sunlight near the windows. It was a large table, round and topped with creamy rose-veined marble. She opened one of its several shallow drawers and removed a pipe and a pouch of tobacco.

The pipe was not at all what he imagined. Its bowl should have been black and shaped like the head of a wild horse or an African woman with tight kinky hair and swollen lips and a gold nose-ring, or it should have been chalk-white, the face of a madman or a coolie, or it should have had no shape at all, formless and chaotic. It was not a large pipe, very ordinary-looking, a light reddish-brown in color. When she had sat in her chair before the little fire, she filled the pipe with tobacco from the pouch and lighted it with a kitchen match. It smelled like chocolate, cooking on a stove. Robert sat in the upholstered chair with blue brocade and did not notice whether he felt large or small. Grief was everywhere, but it was hard to form a mental picture of the dead child. He remembered skinning a catfish with his father. With the fish still alive they cut a circle around the head and pulled off the skin, strip by strip, with a pair of pliers. He prayed forgiveness, or tried, and did not feel forgiven. He wanted to be alone. He didn't want to be here with Mrs. Tremble. But if he went back home, across the pasture to his own house, he would be too much alone. He was afraid of what he might do, or become. Mrs. Tremble was talking. He tried not to listen, but it was impossible.

She stopped and puffed at the pipe and struck a new match to goad it to life again. "That was a long time ago," she said. "I was younger then than you are now. That year—one of those years—a man came, an old man, and camped out, right in the middle of town, not so far from my family's house. We called them hoboes back then. There were more of them then, it seems to me. He put up a tepee-like affair, made from—oh, you know—one thing and another. Packing crates, scraps of lumber, an old door from no-telling-where. Right beneath the old railroad trestle." Mrs.

Tremble's voice was odd. There was something in it, like pain, but that was only a part. There was old-lady nostalgia, and obsession, and senility, and yet none of these exactly. Robert believed that later she might not even remember saying these words, telling this tale. Now and then he saw the green bottle, the stain on the floor. He wondered how he could continue to live, knowing he had killed his brother. He wondered what his father must be feeling. For the first time he thought of suicide.

"Everyone talked about the hobo," Mrs. Tremble went on. "Children sometimes slid down the clay embankment to his tepee and sat with him. I did so myself. He was kindly, and he stank, of course. I think now he must have stolen food to stay alive. I'm not really sure. People might have given him things. He called himself a 'Sin Eater.' No one knew what he meant, or cared, I suppose. There were so many odd ones . . . " She blew a long stream of smoke through the firescreen, and the hot coals flamed up and danced.

"Someone died not long after, a few weeks after we first noticed him. It was a woman, some old woman. I don't even remember her name, I only remember it was the first funeral I ever went to.

"It was held in the old lady's home. That was the way then, the corpse laid out—'decently,' was the expression—for viewing. People came and brought things. There were covered dishes of food, and a bottle of bourbon in the linen closet. The men drank from it—discreetly they must have imagined. Afternoon changed to dusk, and dusk to night, and most of us were still there.

"There was a knock at the kitchen door. It was not a thing you would expect. Persons either come to a wake or they don't, you know. No one comes so late, or to the back door. When someone finally heard and went to answer it, it was the hobo, the man who called himself the Sin Eater. His face was yellow-looking, probably from jaundice; so many of the old-time ones were sick, or alcoholic. He was wearing a dark coat of some kind, and probably nothing else. His legs and feet were bare. He stank terribly, an odious, leathery old man. But something about him—something

about the outrage of his coming to that house, at such a time—
caused my father and the rest not to send him away just then.
They opened the screened door and he came in."

Mrs. Tremble let out a small, mirthless laugh, bewildered almost, and bewildering. Robert was careful not to be struck by her
breath. "The house grew quiet," she went on. "He came farther
in, and the crowd parted to let him pass. Food was spread along a
makeshift counter in the kitchen, put together out of boards and
saw horses. Butterbeans and crowder peas and fried squash, all
the rest, a typical wake in a little southern town. Somebody had
brought a ham.

"The Sin Eater looked at the food. He had a quiet, ordinary
voice. We had not expected that, somehow, even those of us who
had talked with him. 'Put some in a bowl, please'm,' he said, almost shy, 'a wood bowl if you have it.' One of my aunts, a large-
breasted woman with her slip always showing, did as he said.
She put a little of each food, one thing right on top of another, in
a big maple salad bowl. I thought he was just begging. Everybody
thought so, probably. We were all terribly embarrassed, even outraged, I suppose. All we wanted was for him to be gone and for
this to be over. But you couldn't help feeling sorry for him.

"The food, all the juices, mingled together in the bowl. My
aunt tried to hand it to him, but he turned and wouldn't take it.
He walked through the house, big as Ike and twice as natural, and
went in the living room, where the old woman lay in her coffin.
It was no more than a pine box, with the lid not yet nailed down.
'I'd be proud to receive it now,' he said, meaning the bowl of food.
He wanted it handed across the corpse. I'll never forget his quaint,
countrified way of speaking. He'd be 'proud to receive it.' Some
of us children giggled behind our hands.

"He took the bowl from my aunt and held it over the corpse,
just for a moment. He placed the bowl upon the dead woman's
breast. Why on earth he was allowed to do such a thing, I will
never understand. Old men like him were never really welcome
in town, certainly not in our homes. Why didn't someone say,
'Well, now, wait just one minute here'? Some red-faced man,

maybe, like my father. No one said anything, though. Not a word. Then, with no utensil except his filthy hands, he ate the food, every morsel, right over the woman's corpse. Can you believe such a thing? When he had finished, he burned the bowl in the fireplace with fat pine. We just stood there, men, women, and children. It was all we could do, just stand there looking like fools. All of a sudden he was speaking again. It was still the same countrified, untutored voice but different now, not affected at all but slightly more distant, more formal and yet more filled with passion. 'I am the Sin Eater,' he said. 'I am the propitiation for your sins. I have taken unto my flesh all the sin and guilt of these here assembled, and especially those of the woman who lies dead before me. I am unclean with them. I feel them. They burn inside me. Despise me, and beware of me. Touch nothing of me, neither of my body nor of my clothing. Azezial rages inside me. I am the Sin Eater, and I am doomed.'

"By now, of course, the outrage could not be ignored. Several men—probably most of them had drunk an extra share at the linen closet by now—ushered him roughly out the back door and warned him not to show his face around here again. Maybe he had better get moving, get on out of town, they told him. The next day he was not in the tepee, the little hovel he had set up beneath the trestle. When he still failed to show up that night, the tepee was dismantled and burned."

Mrs. Tremble lighted the pipe again and blew out the match with smoke. A sickening cloud of her effluvium seemed to have formed in the air of the room. It was not the pipesmoke itself; that smelled good, like candy. It was something from inside herself, a malodorous, personal stench, that stank up whatever space she occupied. She puffed deeply on the pipe, again and again. Sky rockets of her fetid breath detonated about his head, fulminated in the air. The paint on the walls blistered and cracked and fell away. Plaster crumbled to dust and sifted down into his hair. He was determined to think of his dead brother. The death-pale face, the rolled-up eyes. This beastly old woman! Her boring spew of boring childhood!

Suddenly, he was taken off guard. He had not been looking at her, and while his attention was away, she had moved from her chair and was standing directly above him. Her breath, her filthy, stinking breath, covered him like a sour, damp blanket. He was sick; he began to retch. "I just want you to know how sorry I am, child," she said. "I swan." She bent over and took him in her arms and kissed him with her split, chapped lips. "I'm just so sorry, child."

"Get away from me!" he screamed. He struggled and kicked and flung his arms. He dug his nails into the brocade of the chair and squirmed free, squirting from her bewildered grasp and almost knocking her over. "I hate you!" he screamed. "I hate you! I hate you!" He ran from the room and burst out the back door into the yard. When he had crossed the fence into the pasture, he stopped and looked back. She was at the back door, looking as if she had aged a hundred years in the last sixty seconds. "You stink!" he screamed. "Your breath stinks, and I hate you!"

He turned and ran toward the lake. Goats parted, bleating, fanning out before him. There was a stitch in his side when he stopped, and his breathing was raw and painful. He fell to his knees and gasped for breath. He got up again and ran again until he fell, this time near the lake. He cried, so loud and so strenuous, he wished he could see himself in a mirror. He had never heard such crying. He hated that damned old stinking woman. He hated her.

Later, when he was finished crying, he could not remember having stopped. He may have slept. He was very tired, and he wished his father would come home. He felt the back pocket of his jeans for a handkerchief, but did not have one. He blew his nose with his fingers and wiped his hand on his pants.

He was embarrassed at what he had said to Mrs. Tremble, but he was not sorry. He did hate her. He wondered why he had put up with her for so many years, and why his mother and father had forced her on him. Later, he would apologize, just to keep everyone happy. But he wouldn't mean it, and she would know he didn't.

As he was trying to decide whether to go on and get that part of it over, or whether to sneak across the pasture to his own house, he noticed something in a patch of cane to his right. It was the partly eaten carcass of a baby goat and, just before it sank into the woods out of sight, a glimpse of the black dog he had seen earlier. He was not afraid, exactly, since he knew the dog had eaten; there would be no reason for it to attack. But he did not feel safe enough to stay alone any longer either. He walked up the pasture toward Mrs. Tremble's house.

It was odd, he thought, feeling the cockleburrs and beggars' lice collecting in his socks. It was odd that nothing was changed. It was not like in stories, where people always seem to change. He felt different, of course, emptier, because he had cried; but nothing had really changed. He had learned nothing that would make him, overnight, grow into a man, the way people did in stories. He was not better, or wiser. A brother was dead: that was true. But not even that loss, that diamond of pain and emptiness, could be transformed to abstraction, to innocence, or its loss. The marvel was, in fact, that everything could be so much the same, that what his father said could be true: no blame, no guilt. Life was not a dream, he thought, or a story; the persons you meet are not fabulous, or enchanted. Mrs. Tremble was no witch. The wonder, whether you liked it or not, was the choppy surfaces of lakes and the mounds of fireants and the wild peacocks in the trees. The miracle was the hunger of wild dogs and the availability and vulnerability of goats.

RAT SONG

Missy first approaches us about the rats. They are just the most darling things, she says, and may she bring them home for the weekend, *all* the kids are getting to take care of them over the weekend, and they can't just be left in the classroom to *starve* till Monday, can they, so can't I, please?

Rats? I say. You mean hamsters? or gerbils?

Well, sort of, she says. They're in a hamster cage, and one of the kids in the split section of her learning pod (which I take to mean the sixth grade) donated them, you know, when her father was transferred back to California or somewhere, and now Miss Cheshire, our unit leader (which I understand to mean teacher) is lining up volunteers to keep them on weekends, so can I, please?

Rats? her mother says. You mean mice?

White mice? I say, encouraged.

Well, no, Missy says, not exactly white, but can she?

Oh, I love gerbils, her mother says. They're so educational, and so natural.

Well, I don't know, I say. The fish were one thing—and I have to admit, I say, you're doing a fine job with the fish, feeding them and so on—but white mice, I'm not so sure.

I love the rats, Daddy, she assures me. I love them more than anyone else in the pod, more than the unit leader even, so can't

I, Daddy, please? She will take full responsibility, she swears. Really.

Have you fed the fish today? I say impotently, vanquished with the word *daddy*, the first time she's called me that since her mother decided Roy and Meredith sounded more mature than daddy and mommy.

Missy brings the rats home, two of them. They sit on the top shelf of their yellow plastic hamster cage, motionless. They are rats all right, and not white.

Aren't they beautiful! Missy says.

None of us can disagree with that, her mother says enthusiastically. Their fur, she says, is so thick and glossy, their eyes so—so vulnerable!

I am horrified by them. Everyone looks at me for a statement of approval, so I manage to say, Very attractive pets, but I don't think . . .

Their names are Harriet Tubman and Diphtheria Jean Johnson, Missy tells us, two historical figures her pod has been studying. (*Exploring* is actually the word she uses.)

Hm, kind of super names for gerbils, her mother says seriously.

My God, I think. My idea of boldness in education and child-rearing is letting Missy watch the black mollies give birth in the aquarium.

Oh, this is nothing, her mother assures me in private, as I gulp J&B. You should have been in town last year when Missy's pod went on a field trip to the large animal clinic and helped foal a mare. Bloody hands and all, she assures me.

Well, all right, I think. The rats are in the house for the weekend; there is nothing I can do about that. And in any case, the beasts are caged, and besides that, I tell myself, it's an old prejudice anyway. What if hamsters had been responsible for the plague? Or featured on *Sixty Minutes* as a commentary on inner-city living? What if gerbils lived in barns and sewers and cut chickens' throats and carried rabies? Wouldn't we probably keep rats as pets and buy poison for the others? Yes, but it's the other way around, I reply logically and without feeling much comfort. (It has taken me most of several months to get used to the fish.)

But now the fish, I remind myself, are another matter—I was certainly wrong about the fish. I have indeed grown accustomed to them and have even come to enjoy them, to think them beautiful. Some of them anyway. And it was I who suggested buying the larger tank. Seventy gallons. The same might be true this weekend of the rats. I might become their champion. Well, no, not that, but it will work out, I tell myself, or at least it will be over soon enough and the rats will be back in the schoolroom where they belong. I look into the fish tank and tap lightly on the side of a yellow tin of fish food and watch the flakes drift down through the crystal water like snow. The algae-eater, a rock-colored fish I mistakenly contributed to the collection in a moment of familial zeal, has grown in a relatively short time from the size of a finger joint to a great menacing beast of five or six inches, thick as a cigar. I watch him now, swimming his buzzardly way among the angels and mollies and tetras. He eats not only algae, he has eaten one of the snails, torpedoed it against the glass wall until it released its grip and fell to the bottom of the tank, then ripped away the sticky flesh from its underside and sucked it out. That was months ago. The thought comes back now as the hideous creature settles behind an electronically operated sea chest which pops open every ten seconds and reveals a grinning skeleton.

The rats are placed in their cage on the second tier of a wood-inlaid table near the aquarium. They can be friends with the fish, Missy tells us, and introduces them by name. Oddly enough, the rats do seem interested in the fish. Look, my wife says cheerily, I think they notice each other.

The rats sit on their shelf behind the yellow plastic, glaring at the fish and slowly grinding hunks of wilted lettuce between their teeth.

Maybe they want to go for a swim with their new friends, my wife jokes prettily.

Maybe they want to tear out their gills and drink their cold blood, I try to joke back, but no one laughs. I would gladly give them the algae-eating snail murderer.

Yet, despite my prejudice against the beasts, the rest of the afternoon and evening go fine. Friday. The rats do no more than stare at the fish and eat lettuce. Missy changes the paper in their cage once, very handily and with genuine affection for the creatures inside. She strokes their necks and ears and calls them Harriet and Diphtheria, and sometimes Hattie and Dippy, and the rats respond gently to her touch, not stupidly like gerbils but more like house cats, turning their little heads to direct the passage of her finger over their bodies, then nuzzling their faces into her hand and into each other's neck. Missy accepts their gentle behavior with delight.

You must admit . . . her mother says, looking meaningfully at me and without finishing her sentence.

I admit that, yes, yes indeed . . . with no thought of finishing my sentence either, and head for the liquor cabinet.

And in truth the whole business would be not simply, in my wife's words, an educational experience; it would be tender and touching and sweet, if the creatures were anything less repellent to me than the filthy monsters behind that yellow plastic. Not that they actually appear filthy, or monstrous; they are quite domestic in appearance, their fur does have a healthy look, a sheen. They scratch and lick themselves frequently. Nevertheless, I lie awake listening for them to move. I hear nothing. I prop against my pillows and examine my aversion to rats, bring to memory every rat I have ever encountered.

The memories are few enough and unspectacular: one monster caught in the barn by a large collie on a farm I visited as a child. But that is a good memory for the most part, and at the time I didn't really get a good look at the rat. Another, more recently, peered out of the metal door of a Dempster-Dumpster at the liquor store—momentarily frightening, no more than that. Still another rat, also in my childhood, ate fig preserves in my grandmother's pantry. This memory brings me straight up in bed. The rat cracked the paraffin seal of the jar and dipped out whole figs with its front

feet and slipped them dripping with syrup into its mouth. I turn
on the light and listen for a rustling sound. Jesus, I say aloud, but
hear nothing more than my own cantering auricles and ventricles
and my wife's regular breathing beside me. Daumier's barrister
above the bedroom mantel threatens to gavel out my brains, so I
turn off the light again and lie awake. And in fact the gavel brings
back another childhood memory. Once in an early June my father
was getting the croquet equipment out of the summerhouse in
Old Saybrook when a mouse scuttled across the floor. In a single
wonderful motion, as though the mallet were part of his graceful
arm, he swung in a wide arc and came down directly on the
mouse. It splattered everywhere. But that was a mouse, I remind
myself, not a rat. I listen again and hear nothing. I turn on the
light and pick up a book.

My wife turns halfway over in her sleep and with her creamed
face argues for a face-lift, the promise of one if she should ever
need it. She'll never need it. I stay up alone all night.

Saturday goes much the same. More lettuce, more cage-
cleaning and stroking. When Missy is not handling them, the rats
snuggle contentedly together in the top shelf area and stare at the
fish. After lunch Missy takes them onto the patio and out of the
cage. Settled into the hammock with her head on the pillow, she
allows the rats to crawl over her An Ounce Of Kif Makes You
Feel Like A Camel tee-shirt, which reveals her newly formed and
embarrassingly untrained breasts. It is more education than I can
take, except that all three of them, Missy, Dippy, and Hattie, look
so contented and relaxed. The rats' movements across her little
hillocks are slow and at times comically clumsy, but at the same
time alert and domestic-looking. Harriet scratches behind one ear
with her hind foot, Diphtheria picks a flea out of her fur with an
agile hairless little monkey hand. That afternoon I buy two Sergeant's Sentry IV flea collars and ask Missy please to put them on
the rats and wash her hands. My wife tells me how thoughtful
I'm getting to be. Missy calls me daddy a hundred times a day. I
get the impression she is counting how many, but it makes me
feel good anyway.

Don't the gerbils look cute in their teensie flea collars, my wife wants to know. We should get little tinkle bells for their necks, she believes. Suddenly I feel the way I felt last vacation when I agreed to wear a Have A Happy Day button.

I advise against investing too much money in the rats, since we only have them for the weekend.

How much could two tinkle bells cost? she laughs with a scolding music, and I have to agree that they needn't be silver, need they? and try to laugh a little myself.

Oh, can they be silver, Daddydaddydaddy? Missy says, Oh, please, can they?

Goddamnit.

On Sunday I take the call from Miss Cheshire, Missy's teacher. She sounds drunk. Listen to me, she says with authority, I've been thinking about this rat business all weekend, have been up nights and have looked at the problem from, so to speak, every angle, so understand that this is not just something I thought up today, so anyway, this is the thing, don't bring those rats back to school. I don't want them, and if Missy shows up with them I'm going to send her back home, I'm not going to let her in the schoolroom, so don't try it.

Well, now, wait just one minute, I say, but with no luck, since Miss Cheshire does not stop talking and does not hear me. She is through with the rats, she says, she made a mistake in ever accepting them in the first place, Missy is the only child who's ever been allowed to bring them into her house, none of the other parents would hear of it, and listen to me, sir, she says, I have had the full responsibility for those goddamn rats ever since they showed up. I've had them every weekend and have lied to the pupils that other pupils were taking them home with them, so don't bring them back to school. I am a young woman, youngish, and have plenty of problems without rats, and you might as well know this too, I'm not wealthy like you, no, and never have been, I live well enough, I'm not complaining, but it's not much and it's sure as hell not enough to support two rats as well as myself in

this rattrap garden apartment I live in, but the money is not really
the issue; it's the rats themselves, I don't like rats, I hate them,
not that they've ever done anything to me, in fact these two, Hattie
and Dippy, are wonderful with the children, so there's nothing
personal, but no more, I can't have them in the room another
minute longer.

I think, This woman is insane, and I know also that she will
beat me, that I will end up with the rats, but still I like her, I feel
close to her, I suspect modern education might be improving. I
tell her the story of the fig preserves and of the splattered mouse.
Over the line I hear ice click in a glass and a deep gulp, a fit of
coughing that ends in several sneezes. When Miss Cheshire comes
back on the line she is even more forceful than before.

Don't bring them back, she begins, with renewed vigor, flush
them down the toilet, whatever you want, but I won't take them,
and don't try to impress me with your summerhouse croquet
mallet bullshit because I've got rat stories that will float ice cubes
in your blood and which I could probably sell to *Reader's Digest*
for a great deal of money as true first-person accounts if I chose to
do so, which I do not, and not one of them involves a croquet
mallet.

A new thought almost staggers me with surprise: I'm falling
in love. She is from Mississippi, she says, she has spent her entire
life getting out of Mississippi, where, she says, the first rat in the
history of the world drew breath, and now she is out, not far out
maybe, a Connecticut suburb is not far out but it's out enough,
and she saw plenty of rats when she was in Mississippi, she says,
and she isn't going to see another one, not even to kill it, though
when she accepted them into the classroom, she says, she thought,
well maybe, maybe I can do it, but I can't, I know that now, it's
like your childhood religion, she says. You never get over it but
you don't have to stare it in the face every day, so now it's over,
you've got the goddamn things, you keep them.

Then she tells a story that almost does freeze my blood. Her
father, she says, was a tall, fat, ironic man who drank heavily,
talked through his nose, and carried a loaded gun in his pants,

whose given name on his birth certificate was Big Boy, named, she says, for a tomato vine that grew outside his mother's window when he was born, which his father (her grandfather) chopped down with a sharpened broad-blade cotton hoe because he (the grandfather, a short man, practically a dwarf, she says) swore he'd never again as long as he lived harvest tomatoes on a stepladder, and sometimes I wish, she says, he'd chopped off my daddy's vine too, because when I was just a little girl, about like your own child, like Missy, she says, my daddy took me with him to a roadhouse called Upchurch's Gas and Gro., which had not one gallon of gas nor one loaf of bread nor anything else except some sorry old booths covered with checkered oilcloth and plenty of sorry whiskey and a low ceiling, and he tapped me on the shoulder when we'd been there a while and said, Hun, lookee hyere, just like that, and showed me directly up above us, not one ass kiss from his head, a rat tail as long as a foot ruler hanging out of a crack in the ceiling boards.

Whispering coarsely, I astonish myself: I think I love you, I suddenly say, but she never hears me, never breaks the headlong progress of her story, talking on, the accent and rhythm and image and idiom of Mississippi slipping more and more into control of her voice, the most beautiful thing I've ever heard, great rivers thudding against barge hulls, lynchings and banjos, sheer music.

He reached up over his head, she says, and looped that rat tail once around his index finger and held on, the rat squealing and squalling and running in place, scuttling and scurrying, scrambling, scratching, spinning his wheels, and going nowhere except in a circle with my tall, fat, ironic horse-ass daddy hanging on for all he's worth and laughing until his shoes were full and took, she says, that damn pistol out of his pants, a big nickeled .44 pistol with "Big'un" spelled out in the handlegrip in twenty-four carat gold letters, which meant my mama's mama had to be buried in a cardboard coffin because that's all we could afford, and held that chunk of nickel up to the scrambling rat and blew him into so many pieces, not to mention the board ceiling of the store, that we never again saw two hunks of meat or hanks of hair bigger than the snippet of tail that broke loose and stayed in my daddy's hand when the rest of the rat went through the roof and a trained bluetick hound out the back door, so keep your goddamn rats and your fig preserve rat stories and shove them up your summerhouse ass, but don't send the rats back to me, I don't want them and I'm not taking them. You can keep the cage, free-gratis.

I love you, I say to the dead phone. She has hung up.

We can keep the rats, I tell Missy. I've already discussed it with your teach—ah, your unit leader, and it's all right with her.

My wife tells me how sort of family-oriented I'm proving to be after all and how proud of me she is. Missy burbles to overflowing with daddydaddys. She has special collars made for them and attaches them with sterling silver tinkle bells. The Sergeant's flea collars stay in place but seem to do no good. The rats continue to pick at their breast fur and scratch behind their ears.

I ask my wife if she thinks the scratching means anything.

Like what? she wonders through Cointreau in a manner that assures me of what I already suspect, that I don't know what I'm talking about.

Like, well, I don't know, some disease or something, diphtheria maybe, or, hell, I don't know, bubonic plague, what do I know about rats?

She says I'm overreacting but that I'm a sweet sort of silly thing to think of it and why don't I take the pets to a veterinarian if I'm worried, have him give them a complete checkup. That's the only *sensible* thing to do, she reasons.

Missy takes them in while I sit in the car. They come out with little tags to go on the hooks with their bells, and documents declaring them free of disease and immune from distemper. I doubt they were checked for plague but say nothing.

The rats grow to incredible size, barn rats if there ever were two, as big as house cats, still crouched onto the tiny shelf of the yellow plastic hamster cage, their fibrous ropy tails hanging to the bottom floor of the cage. Their bells don't tinkle. They watch the fish.

The fish start to die, the silver-tipped tetras. Maybe it really is the plague, I think, or the evil eye. Or maybe I'm just going crazy. In any case, I certainly don't seem very sensible. At first I can't know for certain the fish are dying, I can only guess. None but the five tetras seem affected.

Daddy, look, Missy says, feeding them from the fishfood can. The tetras all have their mouths open, aren't they silly?

Oh, Jesus. It's true, all five are swimming around the tank with their mouths locked open. I squat and look at them in horror. They can't live like that, I almost tell her. They can't live with their mouths locked open. But I say nothing.

The fish are dying, I tell my wife later. The tetras.

Oh, well, she says, tetras never last long. We can get more.

No, I say, I mean I think the rats killed them. (This comes as a rather large surprise to me as well as to her, but the moment I say it I almost believe it.)

Whaaaaat? she says, exaggeratedly suspicious. How?

By looking at them, I almost say, by giving them fleas. Instead I say, I'm not sure, they're just doing it. I'm worried.

They don't look dead to me, she says, looking at them. You haven't mentioned this to Missy . . . ?

Certainly not. I drop the subject for now.

The next day the fish are ravenously hungry, and the algae-eater is subdued into hiding behind the grinning skeleton. The tetras are eating every morsel of food in sight, swimming to the top of the tank, diving, feeding, skimming along the surface of the water with their mouths wide open sucking in food. It is obscene. The rats pick at invisible fleas.

Don't feed the fish anymore, I tell Missy. They're sick.

But Missy feeds them more. The other fish will starve, Roy, she says. The greedy old tetras are eating just everything.

Which they are, scooping up every flake into their gaping mouths, no matter how much is poured in. Missy feeds on.

Then the strange movements begin. Without warning the tetras suddenly plummet to the bottom of the tank, then as rapidly flash

upward and leap from the water. After skimming the surface again
for a few minutes they drop again with incredible verticle speed
to the bottom. Then up again, down, all five of them, day and
night, day in and day out for a week, scooping up gargantuan
amounts of food from the surface with their locked-open mouths.
I become a nervous wreck trying to watch them.

I call Miss Cheshire and tell her who I am. Can rats carry
plague? I say into the phone. I mean this to be a joke, but suddenly
it isn't. There is no answer. I notice that I sound a little frantic.
Can rats, I inquire in a bizarre parody of self-control, transmit bubonic plague to fish? (The idea seems ridiculous even to me, but I
fear it nonetheless.) There is a long pause on the telephone as I
wait for her answer.

Finally she speaks: I really wouldn't know, she says, and
hangs up.

The tetras die, all of them. I am the only one who seems to
recognize the possibility of a connection with the rats. I devote
myself to a proof of the connection. I scan a decade of old news-
papers in the city library, I live with the *Reader's Guide* and the
Encyclopedia Britannica. At night in bed I say to my wife, I think
the rats have fleas of the type that carry bubonic plague. (The no-
tion is extreme, as I recognize even as I say it, but I want so badly
to be right about something, anything, that I can believe it.) I've
looked it up, and I'm pretty sure of it. I think the fish died of the
plague, some form of it. I don't know how.

I hope you haven't told Missy that! she says, startled. And
because I haven't even thought of telling her I believe for an instant
I am less of a fool than I am—that I am sensible and winning.

No, I say, I haven't. I think we can just get rid of the rats
quietly, and that will be that. We can get another pet for her.

What! says my wife, astonished.

Maybe the state health office should be the ones to handle this,
I say, feeling more sensible than ever, and well loved. And Missy
should have a complete physical checkup, of course. We all should.

Are you mad? my wife says. When I said I hoped you hadn't

told Missy, she says, I meant I hoped you hadn't jeopardized your credibility with her, because I honestly believe if you can just sort of cool it with a low, and I mean looooow, profile . . .

Look, I say, unable even to wonder that credibility and profiles had got mixed into a conversation about plague and yet pretending to be much calmer than I am in order to preserve whatever insane credibility I might have left, see this newspaper clipping? There were three recorded cases of bubonic plague in Utah last year. Do you realize what that means?

I certainly do, she says, it means Utah is just as unenlightened and filthy as every one has always known it was and has caverns full of bats and God knows what else; besides the gerbils have been checked by the vet.

They are not gerbils, I say evenly, they are rats. I leave the bedroom. And they've got the goddamn plague! I shout back over my shoulder, trembling. And it's New Mexico that has all the bats, not Utah! A geographical victory, I think, seems better than none at all. Besides, the plague theory is becoming enormously important to defend.

In my anger I dial Miss Cheshire. Miss Cheshire, I say, you are, in a primitive way, quite lovely, I suspect, certainly plainspoken in your crudely attractive way, and probably a good teacher, but despite all that, madam, you are a hick, one who—very like my wife, in fact—is self-serving in the extreme, a bully, and profoundly rude. My rats have bubonic plague, and your telephone manners are quite coarse. Goodbye. I slam the receiver.

I wake up Missy. Missy, honey, I say, Harriet Tubman and Diphtheria Jean Johnson have bubonic plague. We've got to get rid of them right away.

Oh, please no, Daddy, she weeps, seeming to come awake immediately, please no, get them shots for it.

Get up.

She pops out of bed in her blue-and-white nighty saying, Please don't kill my friends, don't kill Hattie and Dippy, please. Her devastating loveliness and disarming selfishness remind me of her mother when we met. I press on.

Where did you say that child's father was transferred back to? I say, imagining a rhetorical premise: California is in the West, Utah is in the West, there is plague in Utah . . .

What child? she says.

The kid who gave the school the rats; where was it they lived before coming here?

I don't remember, she says. Utah, I think, or New Mexico, somewhere out West.

Utah, for Christ's sake! I screech, forgetting my premise. It was not Utah; it was California! Wasn't it?

Utah or California, someplace like that, she says.

Missy, listen to me, how in God's name can you confuse Utah and California, honey, which was it?

I don't know, she moans, crying now.

Her mother gets out of bed. What on earth! she says, what are you doing to her?

Trying to save her from bubonic plague, I say, and teach her some geography. (Why, I wonder, has elementary geography assumed such a central importance in this household?) Honey, I say again to Missy, were you dreaming about Utah? Did you hear me talking about Utah in your sleep?

She bawls and won't answer.

Why don't I shut up? I wonder.

Leave her alone! her mother demands.

Look at those goddamn rats, I demand right back, clearing my head of the Golden West and not even bothering to point out that the algae-eater is devouring one of the tetras—there is plenty of other evidence. Harriet Tubman is staggering around in the floor section of the hamster cage, her jaw locked open and her pink tongue lolling out of her mouth. She pants for breath. Diphtheria Jean is on the top shelf doing nothing but looking at the algae-eater.

Well, clearly, I say with justification, the tetras are dead as hell. I dip out the four-and-a-half remaining ones from the tank in a little net and hold them as I speak, droplets of water darkening the maroon sparrow in the rug. And, I continue, can anyone deny

that Harriet Tubman is seriously ill? (No one can.) That she is un-
usually clumsy and her jaw is locked open? (The same.)

Animals die of a thousand things, says my wife sensibly.

Is lockjaw part of the bubonic plague? Missy says.

No, not that I know of, I admit, probably not.

Can fleas bite fish?

No, I say. No, of course not.

Well, there you are, her mother concludes, squashing me with
the unspoken remainder of a syllogism.

Still, I notice both Missy and my wife are impressed, pale and
stunned by the specter of the sick rat. The four-and-a-half fish.

No logic in the world, I conclude, will save that dying rat. I
fling the fish aside and sleep in a guest bedroom.

Harriet Tubman dies the next day with her gaping mouth
rested across her right foreleg and a slab of lettuce beneath her
belly. Her eyes are wide open as a fish's. Missy and her mother are
silenced by the death. I can scarcely feel good for seeing them so
humbled. I think they might respect me.

Then contagion becomes a problem. Diphtheria Jean stumbles
as she comes down from the top shelf. Her breathing seems
strained. Missy, I say, come look at this. She comes down the
stairway holding the rosewood bannister and limping slightly. My
heart leaps. I'm afraid to mention the limp, afraid my words will
intensify the disease as surely as they have conceived and already
begun to spread it. The thought is inescapable: through my skillful
argument my daughter has contracted black death. Jesus. Is that
possible?

What is it, Roy? Missy asks.

Look, I say at last. Look at Dippy. See how clumsy? That's
how it starts. See how hard it is for her to walk?

Missy is haggard, puffy about the eyes. Missy, are you all right?
She seems feverish and distracted.

Honey, sit over here, no here, on the couch, lie down. I want
to look at you. Where is your mommy, I say, probing deeply into
her groin for the telltale swellings of the lymph glands.

She's in bed, Missy says, she doesn't feel well, and, Daddy,
I'm so sleepy.

I carry her to bed.

The next day Diphtheria Jean dies. No one cares. My wife has
a temperature of 102 degrees, Missy is flushed and too listless to
get up. I take them to the hospital emergency room, where a doctor sees the two of them.

A virus, he thinks. If your wife's fever goes higher, the doctor
says, please do call me. Otherwise I see no reason for alarm. I've
treated dozens of similar cases recently. It comes on suddenly, but
it doesn't last long, he assures me.

When I mention bubonic plague and tell him about the rats
and fish, he laughs. Check with the vet, he says. Or the pet shop.
Plague isn't a virus anyway, he says. It's bacteria. It would have
shown up in the white-cell count. He laughs a great deal and
shakes his head. Plague, I think I hear him say, blowing his nose
vigorously into a handkerchief, bubonic plague. When I ask what
other patients he has treated, what schools the children are in, he
ignores me.

He refuses to hospitalize Missy. She's probably coming down
with the same thing as her mother, he says. It's never as severe
in children.

I consider changing doctors but do not. I take both of them
home and put them to bed beneath down comforters. I go to the
kitchen for aspirin and lemonade, thankful I've not given them
a dread disease after all. If it's true I haven't. No argument, even
between a man and a woman who are no longer in love, should
end in black death. Both are already asleep when I reach their
rooms with the lemonade.

The phone rings. It is Miss Cheshire, speaking with an ice cube
in her mouth, apologizing, as I finally understand, for her earlier
manners.

Take that ice cube out of your mouth so I can understand you,
I say, though I am touched by her call. It is, as far as I can remember, the first time anyone has ever apologized to me. A woman

anyway. Not removing the ice cube, or even apparently hearing me, she wonders if I might come over for a while this afternoon. Her apartment is on Maple, she explains, serving me the address over ice. One of the garden apartments, she says. It's really nice.

I decide I rather like the ice cube after all.

She wants to discuss a compromise of some kind, she says. About the rats. She feels guilty, she says, for her irresponsibility in this matter. And especially, she says, about my rudeness to you. And in a delicious icewarm whisper into my earpiece tells me I am a generous and very forceful man, and please do call her Fanny. She hopes I don't hold any of this against her, she's been a little desperate these past weeks, she sighs. It's a lonely, lonely place, the East, for a country girl.

I don't tell her the rats are dead. Not yet. I don't even tell her I love her, though I do again. No, I think, maybe I don't. No, of course I don't. Not exactly.

I hang up and wonder whether I should take a little gift, a peace offering, some type of counterapology. Something for the classroom maybe, an ant farm. I knot a fresh tie and stand at the hall mirror to catch the three-quarter frontal pose. One hand on a hip, the other hooked carelessly by the thumb in my jacket pocket. Not exactly what I'd hoped: a parody of the Jack Nicklaus men's casuals advertisement. A little ridiculous, but not bad. Not at all. In fact, I look pretty damn good. I unbutton the jacket and quick-flash the red lining at the mirror. Or maybe she would like an amusing little wine, I think. Perhaps a single flower.

WHEELCHAIR

Winston Krepps had been abandoned by his attendant, and the
door was shut tight.

Winston pressed the control lever of his chair. The battery was
low, so the motor sounded strained. The chair turned in a slow
circular motion; the rubber tires squeaked on the linoleum floor of
the kitchen.

For a moment, as the chair turned, Winston saw two teen-aged
boys on a bridge. Winston released the control lever, and the chair
stopped. The boys were naked and laughing, and the Arkansas
sky was bright blue. Winston recognized himself as one of the two
boys. He pushed the hallucination away from his eyes. It was the
day real life had ended, he thought.

The clock above the refrigerator said four—that would be
Thursday. Harris, his attendant, must have left on Monday.

Winston turned his chair again and faced the living room. He
saw a boy lying on his back on a white table. Winston turned his
head and tried not to see. Doctors and nurses moved through the
room. The prettiest of the nurses stood by the table and chatted
with the boy. The boy—it was Winston, he could not prevent
recognizing himself—was embarrassed at his nakedness, but he
could not move to cover himself. An X-ray machine was rolled
into place. The pretty nurse said, "Don't breathe now." The boy

thought he might ask her out when he was better, if she wasn't too old for him. He had not understood yet that this was the day sex ended. Winston looked away and pressed the lever of the chair.

The motor hummed and he rolled toward the bedroom. The tires squeaked on the linoleum, then were silent on the carpet. The motor strained to get through the carpet, but it did not stop. Monday, then, was the last day he was medicated.

Winston negotiated the little S-curve in the hallway. He could see into the bathroom. The extra leg-bag was draped over the edge of the tub, the detergents and irrigation fluids and medications were lined up on the cabinet. Winston saw his mother in the bathroom, but as if she were still young and was standing in the kitchen of her home. He saw himself near her, still a boy, strapped into his first wheelchair.

He closed his eyes, but he could still see. His mother was washing dewberries in the sink. There were clean pint Mason jars on the cabinet and a large blue enamel cooker on the stove. His mother said, "The stains! I don't know if dewberries are worth the trouble." Winston watched, against his will, the deliberateness of her cheer, the artificiality of it.

He stopped his chair in the bedroom. There was the table Harris had built, the attendant who had abandoned him. Harris had been like a child the night he finished the table, he was so proud of himself. He even skipped that night at the country-western disco, where he spent most of his time, just to sit home with Winston and have the two of them admire it together. Winston resented the table now, and the feelings he had had, briefly, for Harris. How could a person build you a table and sit with you that night and look at it, and then leave you alone. It was easy to hate Harris.

He looked at the articles that made up the contents of the room—his typewriter, his lamp, and books and papers, a poem he had been trying to write, still in the typewriter. His typing stick was on the floor, where he had dropped it by accident on Monday.

Then Harris stepped into the line of Winston's vision. Winston had not realized you could hallucinate forward as well as back, but he was not surprised. It was the same worthless Harris. "I'm a boogie person, man," Harris seemed to explain. He was wearing tight jeans and no shirt, his feet were bare. He was tall and slender and straight. "I'm into boogie, it's into me." Winston said, "But you built me a table, Harris." Then he said nothing at all.

Winston's hunger had stopped some time ago, he couldn't remember just when. He knew his face was flushed from lack of medication. His leg-bag had been full for a couple of days, so urine seeped out of the stoma for a while. It had stopped now that he was dehydrated.

Winston heard cars passing on the paved road outside his window. He had cried out until his voice was gone. He imagined bright Arkansas skies and a sweet-rank fragrance of alfalfa hay and manure and red clover on the wind from the pastures outside town. He thought of telephone wires singing in the heat.

Winston looked back at the floor again, at his typing stick. The stick made him remember Monday, the day Harris left, and before Winston knew he was abandoned.

He had been in his chair at the kitchen table with his plastic drinking straw in his mouth. He was sipping at the last of a pitcher of water. The time alone had been pleasant for him—none of Harris' music playing, none of his TV game shows or ridiculous friends and their conversation about cowboy disco and girls and the rest. Winston sipped on the water and felt the top of the plastic tube with his tongue.

He pressed his tongue over the hole in the tube and felt the circle it made there. He thought he could have counted all the tastebuds enclosed within the circle if he tried. He thought of his father holding a duck call to his lips to show Winston how to hold his tongue when he was a child, before the accident. Winston remembered taking the call from his father's hand, and he wondered if that touching were not the last touch of love he had felt—the last in the real world anyway, and so the last. The touching of the tube to his tongue brought his father back to him, the smell of alligator grass in the winter swamp, a fragrance of fresh tobacco and wool and shaving lotion and rubber hip-waders, and more that he had forgotten from that world.

He had gone to his typewriter, and had meant to write what he remembered. He had almost been able to believe it would restore him, undo what was done.

He had rolled up to the table, as close as the chair would take him. The stick with the rubber tips was lying on the table with four or five inches sticking out over the edge. Winston used his single remaining shoulder muscle to push his left hand forward onto the table. His fingers had long ago stiffened into a permanent curl. He maneuvered the hand until the typing stick was between his second and third fingers.

At last he dragged it close enough to his face. He clenched one end of the stick between his teeth and tasted the familiar rubber grip. He steadied himself and aimed the stick at the *on* button of his typewriter. The machine buzzed and clacked and demanded attention. For an instant, as he always did when he heard this sound, he felt genuinely alive, an inhabitant of a real world, a real life. And not just life—it was power he felt, almost that. Writing— just for a moment, but always for that moment—was real. It was dancing. It was getting the girl and the money and kicking sand in the face of the bully. He began, letter by letter, to type with the stick in his mouth.

When he had finished, what he had written was not good. The words he saw on the page were not what he had meant. What he had felt seemed trivial now, and hackneyed. He said, "Shit." He touched the *off* button and shut the typewriter down.

He tried to drop the stick from his mouth onto the table again, but the effort of writing had exhausted him. The stick hit the table, but it had been dropped hastily, impatiently, and it did not fall where Winston had intended. It rolled onto his lap, across his right leg, where he could not reach it. Finally it rolled off his leg and onto the floor.

That was on Monday. He could have used the stick now to dial the telephone.

There was a series of three muscle spasms. The first one was mild. Winston's left leg began to rise up toward his face. The spasm

continued upwards through his body and into his shoulders. For a
moment he could not breathe, but then the contraction ended and
it was over. His foot settled back into place. He caught his breath
again.

When the second spasm began he saw the center of hell. A
great bird, encased in ice, flapped its enormous wings and set off
storms throughout all its icy regions. In the storms and in the
ice was a chant, and the words of the chant were *Ice ice up to
the neck.*

Winston's legs, both of them this time, rose up toward his face
and hung there for an eternity of seconds. He watched the ice-
imprisoned bird and listened to the chant. His legs flailed right and
left in the chair. Now they settled down. They jerked out and
kicked and crossed one another and flailed sidewise again. Winston's feet did not touch the footrests and his legs were askew. His
shoulders rose up to his ears and caused him to scrunch up the
features of his face and to hold his breath against his will.

Then it ended. He could breathe again. It was easy to hate his
useless legs and his useless arms and his useless genitals and his
insides over which he had no control. He was tilted in his chair,
listing twenty degrees to the right.

Winston felt an odd peacefulness settle upon him. He saw a swimming pool and a pavilion in summertime. The bathhouse was
green-painted, and the roof was corrugated aluminum. He saw
himself at sixteen, almost seventeen. For the first time he did not
avert his eyes. A radio was playing, there was a screech of young
children on a slide. The boy he watched stood at the pool's edge, a
countryboy at a town pool, as happy as if he had just begun to
live his life inside a technicolor movie.

There was a girl too, a city girl. She told him she was from
Memphis, her name was Twilah. There was a blaze of chlorine and
Arkansas sun in her hair and eyes. No one could have been more
beautiful. Her hair was flaming orange, and a billion freckles covered her face and shoulders and breasts, even her lips and ears.

The radio played and the sun shone and the younger children screeched on the slide.

Outside his window, where he could not see it, a bird made a sound—a noise, really—an odd two-noted song, and the song caused the memory to grow more vivid, more heartbreaking. He wanted to see all the places Twilah might hide her freckles. He wanted to count them, to see her armpits and beneath her finger-nails and under her clothing. He wanted to examine her tongue and her nipples and forbidden places he could scarcely imagine. It was easy to fall in love when you were sixteen, almost seventeen, and a lifeguard was blowing a steel whistle at a swimmer trespass-ing beneath a diving board.

The third spasm was a large one. It seemed to originate some-where deep in his body, near the core. The tingle in his face that signaled it was like a jangle of frantic bells rung in warning.

He imagined great flocks of seabirds darkening the air above an island. He saw wildlife scurrying for shelter.

Motion had begun in his body now. His legs were rising as if they were lighter than air. Then, suddenly, and for no reason—it may have been merely the nearness of death—Winston did not care what his legs did. He watched them in bemusement. For the first time since the accident, they were not monstrous to him, they were not dwarfish, or grotesque. They were his legs, only that. For the first time in seventeen years, he could not discover—or even think to seek—the measure of himself, or of the universe, in his limbs. He was in the grips of a spasm more violent than any-thing he had ever imagined, in which, for a full minute he could not breathe at all, could not draw breath, and yet he felt as refreshed as if he were breathing sea air a thousand miles from any coast.

He began to see as he had never seen before. He saw as if his seeing were accompanied by an eternal music, as if the past were being presented to him through the vision of an immortal eye. He was not dead—there was no question of that. He was alive, for a little longer anyway, and he was seeing in the knowledge that there is greater doom in not looking than in looking. He fixed his eye— this magical, immortal eye—on a swamp-lake in eastern Arkansas.

In the swamp he saw a cove, and in the cove an ancient tangle of briars and cypress knees and gum stumps. He saw water that was pure but blacker than slate, made mirrorlike by the tannic acid from the cypress trees, and he saw the trees and skies and clouds reflected in its surface.

The eye penetrated the reflecting surface and saw beneath the water. He saw a swamp floor of mud and silt. He saw a billion strings of vegetation and tiny root systems. He saw fish—bright bluegills and silvery crappie, long-snouted gar, and lead-bellied cat with ropy whiskers. He saw turtles and mussels and the earth of plantations sifted there from other states, another age, through a million ditches and on the feet of turkey vultures and blue herons and kingfishers. He saw schools of minnows and a trace of slave-death from a century before. He saw baptizings and drownings. He saw the transparent wings of snake-doctors, he saw lost fish stringers and submerged logs and the ghosts of lovers.

He saw the boat.

The boat was beneath the surface with the rest, old and color-less and waterlogged. It was not on the bottom, only half-sunk, two feet beneath the surface of the swamp.

The boat was tangled in vegetation, in brambles and briars and the submerged tops of fallen tupelo gums and willows. It was tangled in trotlines and rusted hooks and a faded Lucky 13 and the bale of a minnow bucket and the shreds of a shirt some child took off on a hot day and didn't get home with.

The world that Winston looked into seemed affected by the spasm that he continued to suffer and entertain. Brine flowed into freshets, ditches gurgled with strange water. The willows moved, the trotlines swayed, the crappie did not bite a hook. Limbs of fallen trees shivered under the water, muscadine vines, the sleeve of a boy's shirt waved as if to say goodbye. The gar felt the move-ment with its long snout, the cat with its ropy whiskers, the

baptized child felt it, and the drowned man. The invisible movement of the water stirred the silt and put grit in the mussel's shell.
The lost bass plug raised up a single hook as if in question.

And the spasm touched the half-sunken boat.

Winston was breathing again, with difficulty. He was askew in
his chair, scarcely sitting at all. He thought his right leg had been
broken in the thrashing, but he couldn't tell. He wasn't really
interested. He knew he would see what he had been denied—what
he had denied himself.

He watched the boat beneath the surface. The boat trembled in
the slow, small movement of the waters. The trembling was so
slight that it could be seen only by magic, with an eye that could
watch for years in the space of this second. Winston watched all
the years go past, and all their seasons. Winter summer spring fall.
The boat trembled, a briar broke. Oxidation and sedimentation
and chance and drought and rain, a crumbling somewhere, a falling away of matter from matter. In the slowness the boat broke
free of its constraints.

It rose up closer to the surface and floated twelve inches beneath
the tannic mirror of the lake.

The boat could move freely now. Winston was slouched in his
chair, crazed with fever but still alive. He knew what he was
watching, and he would watch it to the end.

Harris said, "I didn't know you would *die*, man. I never knew
boogie could kill anybody." It was tempting to watch Harris, to
taunt him for his ignorance, his impossible shallowness, but Winston kept his eye on the boat.

The boat moved through the water. It didn't matter how it
moved, by nature or magic or the ripples sent out by a metaphor-
ical storm, it moved beneath the water of a swamp-lake in eastern
Arkansas.

It moved past cypress and gum, past a grove of walnut and
pecan. It moved past a cross that once was burned on the Winter
Quarters side of the lake, it moved past Mrs. Hightower's lake
bank where the Methodists held the annual picnic, past the spot
where a one-man band made music a long time ago and caused

the children to dance, it moved past a brown and white cow drinking knee-deep in the Ebeneezer Church's baptizing pool. It moved past Harper's woods and a sunken car and a washed away boat dock. It moved past the Indian mound and past some flooded chicken houses, it moved past the shack where Mr. Long shot himself, it moved past the Kingfisher Café.

And then it stopped. Still twelve inches beneath the water, the boat stopped its movement and rested against the pilings of a narrow bridge above the lake. On the bridge Winston could see two boys—himself one of them—naked and laughing in the sun. Winston did not avert his eyes.

The boys' clothes were piled beside them in a heap. One of the boys—himself, as Winston knew it would be—left the railing of the bridge.

It was part fall, part dive—a fall he would make the most of. It lasted, it seemed, forever. Slow-arching and naked, spraddle-legged, self-conscious, comic, bare-assed, country-boy dive.

There was no way for him to miss the boat, of course. He hit it. The other boy, the terrified child on the bridge, climbed down from the railing and held his clothes to his bare chest and did not jump.

He only had to see it once.

And yet it was not quite over.

Winston's life was being saved, like cavalry arriving in the nick of time. This was not an hallucination, this was real. There was an ambulance team in the little apartment, two men in white uniforms. It was hard to believe, but Harris was there as well—Harris the boogieman, repentant and returned, still explaining himself, just as he had in the hallucinations. "Boogie is my *life*," he said, as the ambulance team began their work.

Then it began to happen again, the opening of the magical eye. It was focused on Harris. Through it he saw, as he always saw, even without magic, the bright exterior of Harris' physical beauty—his slenderness and sexuality and strength and straight back and perfect limbs, and also, somehow, beyond his beauty, which before this moment had been always a perverse mirror in which to view only his, Winston's, own deformity and celibacy and loss, beyond the mirror of his physical perfection and, with clear vision, even in this real but dreamlike room, filled with a hellish blue-flashing light from outside, and with I-V bottles and injections and an inflatable splint for his leg and the white of sheets and uniforms and the presence also of the apartment manager who had come, a large oily man named Sooey Leonard, he saw past Harris' beauty to the frightened, disorganized, hopeless boy that Harris was. Winston understood, at last, the pain in what Harris told him. Boogie is my life. It was not a thing to be mocked, as Winston had so recently thought. It was not a lame excuse for failure. What was terrifying and painful was that Harris knew exactly what he was saying, and that he meant, in despair, exactly what he said. It was acknowledgment and confession, not excuse, a central failure of intellect and spirit that Harris understood in himself, was cursed to know, and to know also that he could not change, a doom he had carried with him since his conception and could look at, as if it belonged to someone else. The knowledge that Harris knew himself so well and, in despair of it, could prophesy his future, with all its meanness and shallowness and absence of hope, swept through Winston like a wind of grief. He wanted to tell Harris that it wasn't true, that he was not doomed, no matter the magnitude of the failure here. He wanted to remind him of the table he had built and of how they felt together that night it was finished, when they had sat at home alone together and not turned on the television but only sat and looked at the table and talked about it and then made small talk about other things, both of them knowing they were talking about the table. He wanted Harris to know that the table proved him wrong.

He could say nothing. The ambulance team bumped and jolted him onto a stretcher-table and held the clanking I-V bottles above him.

The sunlight was momentarily blinding as he was wheeled out the door of the apartment and onto the sidewalk. For a moment

Winston could see nothing at all, only a kaleidoscope of colors and shapes behind his eyelids.

And yet in the kaleidoscope, by magic he supposed, he found that he could see Harris and himself. They stood—somehow Winston could stand—in the landscape of another planet, with red trees and red rivers and red houses and red farm animals, and through all the atmosphere, as if in a red whirlwind, flew the small things of Winston's life: the typewriter and the failed poem in it, the battery charger for his chair, and the water mattress and the sheepskin, the chair itself and the leather strap that held him in it, his spork—the combination spoon-fork utensil he ate with—and the splint that fitted it to his hand, the leg-bag and the catheter and the stoma, his trousers with the zipper up the leg, his bulbous stomach, the single muscle in his shoulder, the scars of his many operations, the new pressure sores that already were festering on his backside from so long a time in the chair, his teeth, the bright caps that replaced them when his real teeth decalcified after the spinal break, his miniature arms and legs, the growing hump on his back, his hard celibacy and his broken neck. And the thought that he had, in this red and swirling landscape, was that they were not hateful things to gaze upon, and not symbolic of anything, but only real and worthy of his love. Twilah was there in all the redness, the long-lost girl with the freckles and the orange hair, who for so long had been only a symbol of everything Winston had missed in life and who now was only Twilah, a girl he never knew and could scarcely remember. It was a gentle red whirlwind that harmed no one. His father was there with a duckcall, his mother washing dewberries. The ambulance door slammed shut and the siren started up. Winston hoped he could make Harris understand.

STORYTELLER

It was Wiley Heard talking and cooling his coffee at the same time. "You heard about all them grain elevators blowing up in Kansas, didn't you?" Wiley was a short, wiry one-legged man with a red face and white eyebrows. He was retired head coach of the local football team. He stopped blowing across his coffee and took a long, slurping pull, then held up the heavy cup, like evidence, so everybody could see. One or two of those standing around moved in closer to the marble counter and were careful not to overturn a spittoon. They poured cups for themselves and lay their change on the cash register. "See this?" he said. "It's the best cup of coffee in the entire state of Arkansas. Right here in Hassell's Blank Store. Used to be called Hassell's Drug Store, long time ago. Back before any you boys would remember." They tried not to notice Coach Wiley pour a nip of Early Times into his coffee from a flat bottle he slipped out of his jacket pocket. "Yessir," he said, "Gene Hassell sold the wrong drugs to the wrong man. Two men, in fact. Federal agents pretending to work on a truck for two days across the street, out yonder by the railroad tracks, before they come in for pills. On account of which old Gene's pharmacy license got taken away. And so did Gene, come to think of it, down to the Cummins penitentiary. Couldn't get him in Atlanta. It was all full up that year, I think was the trouble. His wife, poor thing, Miss Eva, I swan. She just painted out the word *Drug* on the sign and held a shotgun up under her chin, bless her time. It was that old twelve-gauge of Gene's that kicked so bad, real old gun, belonged to his daddy and ejected shells out the bottom. Remington, I think it was. She pulled the trigger and shot off her face. The whole damn thing from the bottom up, jaw, teeth, nose, and eyes, and broke both her eardrums. Terrible sight to see, even after the skin grafts. No face at all. Can't see, hear, smell, or taste, just keep her alive in a nursing home down in Arkadelphia, feeding her through tubes, and not one pellet touched her brain. It's a sad case, boys. It would break your heart. We been calling it Hassell's Blank Store ever since, and him still in jail, I guess, or dead, but you say you did hear about them grain elevators, didn't you?"

Somebody said he had. Everybody else agreed.

"I know you did," said the coach. "You heard about it on the Walter Cronkite Show, didn't you? They had it on the TV every night for a month, seem like. But I bet you forty dollars you didn't hear what happened the other day over in El Dorado, did you? Just outside El Dorado, I ought to say, over close to Smackover. A dog food factory blew up. That's about like El Dorado, ain't it? Ain't nowhere but El Dorado, and maybe parts of north Missis-sippi, they going to blow up a dog food factory. But you never will hear that one on the Walter Cronkite Show, nayo-siree, and don't need to. The longer they can keep El Dorado, Arkansas, off the national news, or Smackover either one, the better for every-body, is what I say. Hound Dog dog food factory—and three men are missing, so they tell me. Might of been mule skinners, mightn't they? I think they was, in fact. If any you boys are look-ing for work they going to need somebody to skin them miserable old horses before they can put them in a can. Over this side of El Dorado actually, up close to Smackover. But that was years ago Gene Hassell went to jail. You boys wouldn't remember him, years ago. Hell, he may not be dead now, all I know. Prob-ably is, though. Probably is dead now he can't drink no more of that paregoric. He probably died his second day off that paregoric, didn't he? He'd been drinking it for twenty years. He's been constipated that long. He probably didn't know what to think, did he, down there in Cummins behind them bars, or out on that hot scrabble farm chopping him some prison cotton, when he felt that first urge to go to the bathroom. Hell, he probably died right off, didn't he? Didn't even have to call the dispensary. He probably got him a shit fit and the blind staggers and keeled over with his eyes rolled up. His old crazy paregoric eyes probably looked like the rolled up window shades of Miss Dee's whorehouse on Sunday morning, he was so happy. But not Miss Eva, that's his wife, she's not dead. She's still over to Arkadelphia at the Wee Care Nursing Home, got a married daughter out in California, or is it grand-daughter, pays the bills. That little red brick building with the neon sign saying Wee Care out on the old airport road, real nice place, and expensive too. But Jerry Rich down in Prescott, out beyond Prescott really, just this side of Delight, he's the one owns this place now, Hassell's Blank Store. He's owned it for years. Poor old woman had to sell out right away, of course, after she lost so much face here in town trying to kill herself, and her husband in the pokey. The daughter had to sell, I mean. And no face at all, Miss Eva, and never did have much personality to speak of. But old Jerry, he doesn't get up here much any more, long as there's a quail in them cornfields and one old sorry dog in the pen. Not even to change the name on the front of the store. Painting out Gene's name would be a piss-pore way to remember a good man, though now wouldn't it? Lord, but his wife was a boring woman, even back when she had a face. It was three of them missing, though, three skinners, all of them white men, I believe it was, I'm not real sure about that. Dog food factory over in El Dorado, outside El Dorado really, out close to Smackover, Hound Dog dog food factory."

Wiley was still talking. "They used to feed dog food to circus animals. Sounds awful, don't it? But it's true. It'd make them crazy, too. It'd make a trained beast turn on his master, so I hear. Nothing to be done about a bitch elephant once they turn on their keeper. Bull elephant's a different story, trustworthiest old wrinkled buggers you ever want to meet, but not a bitch, you can't trust one with a nickel change once she gets sour on life, might as well save yourself the trouble."

"Why's that, Coach Wiley?" The coffee drinkers turned and looked. It was Hydro, a gawky young man with a broom and a large head.

"Nobody knows," said the coach, "and don't ask no more questions, Hydro. Godamighty. You get on done with that sweeping before you start asking so many questions. But it happened one time over in Pocahontas. One two y'all might be old enough to remember it. Your daddies'd be old enough. Some little off-brand circus or other. Clyde Beatty or something. Naw, not even that good. They had two old scrawny lions that hollered half the night they was so hungry from eating that dried dog food they give them. Probably Hound Dog dog food, when they was looking for meat, like that place blew up over past El Dorado, except that factory wasn't there till ten years ago, so it must have been some other brand the lions had to eat, but nobody ought to feed dog food to a lion and get away with it. King Jesus jump down. It'd take a worthless sumbitch to do that, now wouldn't it? Worthless as a whistle on a plow, as my poor old dead daddy used to say. Daddy he was a funny little quiet man with rusty hair and deep eyes. Housepainter and paperhanger, and a good one too, and a handful of elephants with their nose up each other's ass like a parade and some scrawny old woman in a little white dress and bleached-out hair riding on top of the first elephant, when this baggy old gray African elephant went kind of crazy. *Commercial-Appeal* said she was in heat and real nervous. That's when they dangerous. Some old boy name of Orwell, from West Memphis or Forrest City or somewhere, was quoted as saying that was right. He claimed to know all about elephants, though I can't say I ever knew a family of Arkansas Orwells. Plenty of them in Mississippi, of course, Delta people, but none to my memory in Arkansas. Unless, of course, they come here since the World War, but I think she was just sick of Pocahontas and circus food. That'd be me. Best thing ever happened to Pocahontas was that

tornado in 1957, tore down half the town. They just about due
another one, if you want my personal opinion. Didn't have many
teeth, my daddy, and had fainting spells on top of that, because
you notice she didn't bother to pick out her own trainer to step
on. That'd be too easy. She had to bring down all hell and her left
front foot on another African, one of her own people, you might
say. She had to step on some little local boy hired on as a handler.
Plez Moore's grandson is who it was, in case some y'all are old
enough to remember Plez. Course my daddy always did love his
whiskey and had a heart enlarged up the size of a basketball, but
the fainting spells commenced long before that come to pass, who
I always liked, Plez I'm talking about, and hated to see anything
bad come to him in spite of not especially blaming the elephant
and never could straighten up his back, Plez, on account of getting
syphilis when he was just a boy, stepped right on that poor little
child and flattened him out like one them cartoon pictures when a
steamroller runs over somebody. He looked like a pitiful little
black shadow some child lost. But you couldn't blame the elephant, I couldn't, having to live cooped up in Pocahontas all week
and that terrible sawed-off circus. It wouldn't do, though, but
they had to kill the elephant, and you can see their point, especially
if that Orwell boy from West Memphis knew what he's talking
about, though I still think he was from somewhere over in Mississippi.

"Anyhow, that's what the mayor and aldermen said, got to
destroy the elephant. They was agreed with by the Colored Ministers Association, which has now got some other name and is
joined up with the NAACP. They was quickly agreed with, I
might add, which was the first and last time the Pocahontas town
officials and the colored ministers ever agreed on anything, except
maybe last year when Horace Mayhan—you remember him playing football right here in town and always stunk real bad, before
old man Mayhan moved them all to Pocahontas where they'd
belonged all along and fit in so good with the paper mill—last year
when old Horace won a free trip, so to speak, to Washington,
D.C. He had to testify before a senate subcommittee on the subject

of who cut them eyeholes into the sheets the FBI found in the trunk of Horace's car, that cream-colored Mustang with the rusted top and STP stickers on the front bumper. That boy gave new meaning to the word *white-trash*, not to mention who sawed the stocks and barrels off all his shotguns and enough dynamite to provide every man, woman, and child in Arkansas fish dinner every night for a week. But the trouble was, of course, that nobody in Pocahontas had a gun big enough to kill an elephant, not even a hungry old scrawny elephant that probably needed killing."

"Shoot him in the eye." The words were totally unexpected, but the minute they were in the air everybody knew it was Hydro again and that he was in trouble. He had forgotten that the coach told him to stay quiet. It was obvious from his enormous face that he thought he had made a good suggestion. The coach stopped talking and looked at him. Everybody else looked at the floor and tried not to breathe. They wanted to become invisible. "Hydro, my man," Coach Wiley said, with a chill in his voice that galvanized every gaze upon the floor, "I always kind of liked you, boy. And I know you got your own problems. But listen here. Don't you never interrupt me again. Not now, and not never. Not till you get smart enough to know a whole hell of a lot more about elephants than shoot him in the eye."

"Or," said a voice with an unnatural cherriness, "maybe you could just shoot him up the butt." It was Hydro again, and he had missed the fury underlying the coach's tone. If any of those standing around the coach in the Blank Store had not been too embarrassed to think of it, they might have hated Hydro, and themselves, and they might have hated God for making Hydro so damn dumb. Nobody thought of it. Nobody knew why they depended on Wiley Heard's approval, and dreaded his disapproval. "It's bound to bust something loose up in there," Hydro said, still pleased as he could be to help.

The coach became more deliberate. For everybody but Hydro, breathing was out of the question. Some of this began to dawn on Hydro.

"Hydro," said Coach Wiley Heard, "I am going to say this one more time. Now, boy, I mean for you to listen. Are you listening?" There was no need for Hydro to answer. He had caught on now. "Shoot him in the eye and shoot him up the butt will not do. Not to interrupt me telling a story, nawsir. And neither will anything else do, to interrupt me telling a story. Are you listening, Hydro? Not nothing that you or anybody else that's going to come into Hassell's Blank Store is likely to think up is going to do to interrupt me. So just forget about interrupting me, boy. At any time, or for any reason whatsoever, with shoot him in the eye or shoot him up the butt or anything else. Now do you understand what I am saying?"

Hydro was quiet and miserable. He said, "Yessir," in a tiny whispery voice. He recognized his chastisement. The act of breathing started up again. Throats got cleared, and feet were shifted. Some of the little crowd looked up.

When the coach finally spoke again, it was not to them, not at first, not exactly. His voice was low and deep and coarse and gravelly, and there was a snort of a humorless laugh behind it. "Shoot him up the butt," they heard him say, almost soundless, and they heard the low, snorting laugh. A few of them laughed a little too; they tried it anyway, the laughter, not loud and not self-confident, and when they heard it, they found no pleasure in its sound. For a few more seconds he let the silence continue. He sweetened his coffee again with Early Times, and they made sure they didn't notice.

When he began again, the tone of his story was immeasurably darker. There were no more self-interruptions, there was no more marshaling of irrelevant detail. The story had become deadly serious and even most of the errors of grammar had disappeared from his speech. If the story were told again, or if it had been told without Hydro's interruption, each person in the store could have imagined it as wonderfully comic, the dark, laughing comedy that underlay every tale he told. But it was not comic now. The elephant he said, would have to be killed. It would have to be killed by hanging. Some let out sounds that might have passed for laughs, but none of them were proud to have done so.

"By now the elephant was quiet," he said. "I saw her led to town by her trainer, a dirty man and sad-faced. The bleach-haired woman was with them, too, wearing a maroon suit and low-heeled shoes, the one who rode the elephant in the parade. The railroad crane and log-chain were on a flat car. The chain was made into a noose and put around its neck. The giant gears started creaking, the crane was lifting. I remember a blind fiddler was in the crowd and a little Indian boy with blue short pants and no shirt high up on the top of a locomotive. The elephant's feet were like the feet of a great turtle. The hind feet brushed the air a scant inch above the cinders in the station yard. When she was up, hanging there, choking, she lifted the wrinkled old trunk straight up and trumpeted one time, one blast to heaven, before she was choked dead. Her back feet, her gray old big turtle feet, were just an inch above the cinders, a little inch."

Those who listened stood, silent, and held their coffee cups without drinking. One man, whose son stood beside him, lay an unconscious hand on the boy's arm and pulled him a little closer to his side. No one knew what to say, or do. For a moment, during the silence, they forgot that Coach Wiley Heard was in charge, in control of the pause. He allowed a few more seconds to pass. They thought of the beast's trumpeting. They did not imagine, even for a second, that the coach's story might be untrue, that he might have made it all up, or adapted it from an older tale, and now maybe even believed it was all true, that it had all really happened on a certain day, to a certain people with bleached hair or sad faces or blind eyes or Indian blood, or any other hair and face and eyes and blood he chose to give them, and that it all happened in a station yard in eastern Arkansas, in a town called Pocahontas. If disbelief crept in, it came like a welcome brother into their company. They poured it a cup of coffee and showed it the sugar bowl and treated it like a friend too familiar to notice. They thought only of the gray feet and the cinders, the little inch between.

Then it was over. The coach released them. With a sudden,

unexpected cheeriness, and maybe even a wink, he said, "You not going to forget what I told you, now are you, Hydro?"

"No sir," Hydro said, certain he would not, but still a little uncertain how to act. The coffee drinkers were able to love Hydro again, and pity him and feel superior to him. He shifted his broom and looked at its bristles. Everybody felt confident and happy. Everybody smiled at Hydro's innocence and at his need for forgiveness.

"Shoot him up the butt!" the coach roared suddenly, merry and hilarious and slapping his good leg. "Shoot him up the butt! Great godamighty!" Now they could laugh. They did laugh, uproarious and long. The coach slapped Hydro on the back and called him son and hugged him roughly against him and shook him by the shoulders. "Shoot him up the butt!" he said again. "Got damn, Hydro, I'm going to have to tell that one on you, now ain't I!"

When the laughter was over and the coach had wiped a tear from each eye with a clean handkerchief, he spoke to Hydro in a voice a little different from the one they had been listening to for most of the day. He said, "Let me tell you about my daddy, son. You'd of liked him. He had to walk on crutches all one winter, he had tonsilitis so bad." They knew now that they could stay and hear this story if they wished, but they knew also that it would not be told to them. They envied Hydro. They wished they were Hydro. They wished they were holding his broom and feeling the coach's warm, alcoholic breath on their faces. "Daddy always smelled like turpentine and Fitch's shampoo," they heard the coach say, as if from a distance. "It's the only place I ever smelled the two in combination. It breaks my heart to remember." There was a pause, a silence of a few seconds. "He carried this little nickel pistol with him," the coach said, thoughtful. "I'll show it to you sometime. A little nickel pistol, with walnut handlegrips."

Hydro was happy. Everybody could see that. There was no reason for anybody else to hang around, though. They eased out by ones and twos.

THE COPPER BALLOONS

When he left for work, his wife said she thought he might be running a slight fever. It didn't matter to Toby McNaughton. He felt wonderful, as if something new and uncommon were about to happen in his life. All the way, on the drive from his mobile home in Siloam Springs, down the highway that led through the deep woods where he sometimes hunted, past the brown-stubble pastures full of rich men's horses, past the low-slung chicken-houses and bluffs and outcroppings, into the sturdy little Ozark city, right through the factory gates, Toby McNaughton felt that today was special. That he himself was special.

The security guard, a uniformed man with a leather-bound clock slung from his shoulder on a strap, checked his pass and waved him through. With the others arriving on the first shift, Toby walked from the parking lot and through the factory doors. Lockers were already clattering, and coffee was being brewed in the break room.

He spun the combination lock and opened the door and put away his jacket. He took out his cap and safety glasses and rubber boots and leather gloves. Why was it a person felt this way? He felt friendly; he spoke to everyone. Girls seemed more beautiful; the factory was a comfortable home. He slammed the locker shut and stood in line at the clock.

In just twelve hours he would be back home again. The memory and sweet taste of his wife Kate remained with him, and the vision of their young son, still asleep in his bed. The raise had come through—just a dime, but that was all right. The company had agreed to Washington's Birthday as a paid holiday. It was a fine day for Toby McNaughton.

He took his card from the rack and slipped it into the clock. Clack, it was imprinted. Sweet overtime, sweet time-and-a-half this afternoon. He checked his mailbox. The factory sounds had already begun, the whine and thump of the drill press and punch press and sanders, the soft electrical music of forklifts humming through the plant, warehouse doors opening, gliding up the trolleys and folding open at the ceiling with a clash.

In his mailbox, he saw what he had forgotten. The thing he should have been expecting, anticipating. His correspondence course had come. The brown package, a large, padded envelope with a neat mailing sticker, lay in the box, his name and the address of the company printed neatly on it. He wanted to tear it open right away, tear the staples loose and reach down into the envelope and take it out immediately. He checked the clock above the business office door and decided to wait. The factory sounds were growing louder now, he knew he had better get his own machines running. Then he would look. "Introduction to Business Finance" was the name of the course. You never could tell—it might lead to something. Toby walked to Screw Machine.

The foreman from last night's dog shift had set the machines, as usual. There was not much to do. Toby checked each breech and threader. He checked the rod troughs and safety lights, then sat on a low stool to slip into his boots and glasses. He opened the breeches and started the machines, one at a time. He listened to the shrill efficiency, as, one by one, they reached the high rpms.

His foreman came in with a cup of coffee. Seven screw machines were running now, on automatic. It was too loud to talk. The other men, who were about Toby's age, in their twenties, were starting their machines also. The foreman indicated with his cup that he would be in the break room in case he was needed. It was the usual beginning of a day.

Toby fed a series of brass rods into the number three, four, and seven machines. The other men did the same on the one, two, five, and six. At the opposite end, new-made screws began piling up in the bins. The fragrance of the warm oil that cooled the machines was delicious. Brass shavings piled up on the floor like gold.

This was the moment of the day when Toby's job seemed most pleasant. With the machines running, he felt completely alone and private. He put oil-filled ear plugs into his ears, to protect against damage, and he entered into what he thought of as a loud, familiar silence, a time in which he spoke to no one and no one spoke to him. There were others nearby, the boys on the other machines, the foreman, who, throughout the day, came in and out, checking equipment. Across the aisle, on the punch press, there was the Indian girl, a teenager, who sometimes caught his eye. There were maintenance men on forklifts, and sometimes an inspector. Mostly, though, there was just himself. His communication with others required only a nod, a glance. The floor vibrated soothingly beneath his feet. The machines were running smoothly.

Toby lifted the brown envelope from a barrel of shavings and rested his safety glasses on his forehead. He sat on a stool in the corner and opened his package.

When he drew out its contents, his eyes would not at first focus properly on the book and packet of study sheets and directions. The text book was a wafer-thin, reddish book in a cloth binding. At the lower right corner was stamped the copper-colored imprint of three small balloons and a gondola depending from them. He opened the book at random and looked inside. He was confused. It was as if he were looking at a foreign language. In fact, he *was* looking at a foreign language—he might as well have been. He closed the book and looked at the title, embossed in coppery lettering on the spine. *A History of the English Language.*

He was not angry, not even particularly frustrated. A computer somewhere had sent him the wrong course. It was not the first time such a thing had happened. There was no promise from the factory's management to promote Toby, no matter how many courses he took—a few more weeks of waiting for the proper course was not really a problem. But he did feel a certain emotion, a certain strangeness, looking at this book, at these instructions and lessons. It was part of the same feeling he had experienced in the morning, a premonition of change. A small sound, a difference in sound, in the machine noise, attracted his attention.

It was Number Three. A screw had jammed in the threader and had caused it to stop, to heat up a little. Toby put his instruction materials aside and unbreeched the rod. It was a simple matter to remove the piece of metal from the threader and feed the rod through again. The screws began again to pile up in the bin, the brass shavings on the floor. He signaled Maintenance to empty his barrels of shavings. When they were done, he swept the shop floor with a stiff broom and started filling the barrels again. He could have signaled one of the other boys to spread sawdust, to soak up the accumulation of oil on the floor—but there was no need. He did it himself. When he was finished, the feeling of strangeness had not left him. He was intrigued by the materials he had found in his envelope. He might have just opened an old chest and found treasure. He sat and stripped the cellophane wrapper from the packet of instructions.

Inside the booklet, in black, was the same tiny imprint of the balloons and gondola. He trembled as he read—it was a section titled "Introduction." He felt he was being spoken to by an actual voice. He wished he could see the face behind the voice. It would be a man in a suit, very old and rich. He would sit at a desk in an office with glass walls, the Great Divide, the blue Rockies, visible behind him. He would lift a pen from the desk top and uncap it. He would write on paper the color of bone. The words would say that language was a vast balloon, three balloons, with a gondola dangling beneath them on silk ropes. It was copper balloons, the thinnest imaginable copper, tissuey and airy and magical enough to float away, immense and weightless, three copper balloons with a gondola beneath, as large as civilization, all past and present. The balloons rose up. In the gondola rode all the company of heaven and earth, all peoples and wars and inventions, all circus animals and trapeze dancers, it carried a million gods and graves, Cochise risen, Helios draped in sunlight (where had he seen this, an illustration in the text, a caption?), he saw flocks and bees and gardens and herds, gatherers and dwarfs and madmen. Toby's mind reeled. He looked back at the page. It had not said that. What had come over him? The words had made his imagination see things that were not there. He felt frightened; he had never been so happy.

He put down the instruction booklet and opened the text. He read words he had never known existed, words he could not pronounce but which pronounced themselves in his mind. He read Northumbrian and Cura Pastoralis and Brunnanburh and the harrowing of hell. He thought of the gondola and of the history of words, the words he had said this morning when he left home, "I love you, Kate," and "I'll see you tonight, honey," and "Kiss the boy for me," and all the rest. He imagined other persons, in other times and nations saying the same words, men in Viking helmets or animal skins or space suits, women in their beauty. He imagined the gondola and the copper balloons, thin as tissues, a cornucopia of words and creatures spilling out, calling out in his own voice.

He looked carefully at the page. He turned the pages slowly. He saw a little poem, four lines of unrecognizable words, beneath them a translation. He read the translation. *A little while the leaves are green; then afterwards they fall to earth; they rot away; they turn to dust.* He thought how true this was, how perfectly true, how like the deep woods in northwest Arkansas, where he hunted squirrels, the small river that ran through them carrying yellow leaves on its surface, the river's sandy banks, animal tracks in the sand, sometimes a wet-muzzled deer, hoof-deep in leaf mold, looking up at him. He thought of the abandoned mill upstream, where, sometimes, he laid his dead squirrels and, with a sharp knife, separated them from their skins and threw the bright guts into the stream. He thought of the concrete foundation, so distant from present civilization that it was not even littered, no charred remains of campfires, no beer cans or rubbers or scrawled names. He thought of the steady music of the spillway, the unrecognizable pieces of rusted machinery that lay near the water, where the mill wheel had been.

" . . . relationships . . . " a voice seemed to say, from nowhere. He turned and almost collided with someone, a person standing scarcely inches away from him, who seemed to have been talking to him for some time. What was going on here? It was Lance Eisen, one of the other men on Screw Machine. How long had he been talking?

"Wait," Toby shouted at him.

It was time to feed the machines again. He took brass rods from the troughs and fed them in. He poured fresh oil through each machine and enjoyed the fragrance, the warmth. Eisen was still talking. Just what was going on here? Nobody talked in this noise. Toby took out an ear plug and moved away from the machine, toward the corner where he had been sitting.

Eisen towered over Toby. He was at least six feet five, with brilliant black hair and eyes. He was crying. Could this be possible? They had never spoken more than a dozen words—just hello and goodbye and do you want some coffee. The heavy doors at Receiving opened, across the plant, and flooded the floor of Main Assembly and part of Screw Machine with sunlight and cold air. A tractor-trailer, loaded with flattened cardboard boxes, backed into the bay, and the great doors closed again.

Toby thought again of the book. He took off his gloves and picked up the book. He thought of Northumbria and the copper balloons. He thought of the ruined mill and the poem of green leaves and decay.

" . . . age . . . it's . . . up," Eisen said, or seemed to say. Toby motioned him to speak directly into his ear. " . . . marriage . . . up," Eisen said.

"Louder," Toby shouted. He gripped his new book and instruction materials tightly in his arms. He felt giddy and flushed.

Eisen was still crying. He shouted into Toby's ear again. Toby was afraid he might be sick. Eisen's marriage was breaking up, Eisen shouted, above the seven screw machines. Toby gave his machines a quick check again, breech, threader, feeder. He checked the oil level. To keep his sanity, he also checked the Indian girl. This time she was not already looking at him. He saw her in profile, the rust-colored skin and fine nose, the high cheekbones. He imagined her on the gondola, beneath the copper balloons. Her hair net, which the women wore for safety, became a beaded band, then full headdress. The machine key, on a string around her neck, became a necklace made of squash blossoms—they made him think of fertility and youth. He saw horses and spears and paint; he saw beehive ovens and pottery and drums. He saw his own son a papoose asleep on a cradleboard, he saw in her the Indian women in his trailer park and from the reservation, toothless squaws shooting pool in the back room of Muskogee beer halls, he saw medicine men in three-piece suits and braves drinking wine from sacks. He heard their language, their drums and chants and smoke clouds, all of them saying, "Northumbrian, Mercian, West Saxon," speaking a harmony of the Gospels, speaking a dream of the Rood, all the strange new words in the Table of Contents he had just read.

He did not want to talk to Lance Eisen. Eisen shouted into his ear, he seemed to say, "Have no fun. Get drunk." Eisen's large hands were cupped directly over Toby's ear now, and he was shouting full strength. All his sentences were chopped short, or seemed to be, like the words of Indians in movies. "Bicycle," he shouted. "Long trip." It was painful, Toby's head was ringing. Eisen was not talking about his wife, he was talking about a young woman he had known briefly in the army. The two of them, along with another couple, had taken a long bicycle trip through Germany. All of them had got drunk the first day out, but Eisen was drunkest. He could not get over the vomiting and diarrhea for two days. "Oh, Jesus!" Toby tried to cry out, but could not. His head was killing him. His emotions had overpowered him, and the noise. He was helpless, he could only listen. He could not get away. The machines screamed and made brass screws. The bins filled with precise, twisted creatures, like sea animals, and the floors with shavings that looked like gold. He could not get away, because he knew why Lance had decided to tell him this.

Weeks ago, Toby had told a navy story in the break room, an adventure on a train in Italy—the hooting diesel, the beautiful Italian sisters who befriended him, the food and wine and sex, the cheesecakes and flowers and fresh fruit. Eisen had loved the story, had taken it to heart and believed every word. Its message was the beauty of sex and adventure, the inseparability of the two. He was judging himself against the story. Toby wanted to get the story back, he wanted never to have spoken the words. The story was a lie.

"I couldn't have screwed her anyway," Eisen was shouting, speaking of the girl in Germany.

Toby shouted back at him, "Lance, I was lying."

He didn't hear. Lance had Toby cornered now, holding his shoulder and weeping and shouting into his ear. "It rained," Eisen said, "turned cold. She got her period."

"Lance, I lied. The Italian girls were a lie."

"She got drunk. Vomited . . . "

The machines pounded and screamed and made screws. Toby tried to pull away. Eisen held him and shouted into his ear.

"We kissed," Eisen shouted, still crying. "All tongues, you know."

"Oh, Christ, help me!"

"Little pieces of vomit—they were down in her throat."

"Mother of God!"

"Sex—it's so awful. Oh, God, it is."

The copper balloons, with the gondola beneath them, tilted and swayed and rose up. The gondola tipped over. It spilled its passengers, terrifying creatures, dwarfs and satyrs and monsters Toby McNaughton could not remember ever having heard of. His wife spilled out, too, his Kate, and himself, as they would be this evening when he got home. They would sit together on the sofa and watch the television news, with their supper plates on their laps. His son spilled out, the baby, as Toby would watch him tonight, sitting in the water of the bathtub, surrounded by toys, a green duck, and a plastic bowl. He would put him in his bed clean and warm and sweet-smelling, wearing crinkled pajamas. They would watch the mobile, made of tiny mirrors in the shape of fish, that hung from the ceiling and sparkled with the last light of evening as it filtered through the windows of his sunny room. He would lie beside him on the bed and prop a bright storybook on his stomach. He would feel grateful never to have to lie to the child, never to hide from him behind a lie. He would hold him close and kiss his still-damp hair, and no words would come between them.

Eisen was still shouting into his ear, his head was ringing with pain. "My wife reminds me of her. I'm impotent with my wife."

Toby McNaughton was shoved into the corner now, all the way against the wall. There was nowhere to go, no escape. Even as Eisen shouted his story, Toby opened the book in his hand, hoping to find the quiet poem, with the green leaves. He could not. His eyes fell, instead, upon a verse from an ancient Bible. The words were magic. There was a translation beneath them, but he understood them already. He could pronounce them, he knew their meaning. He thought of Pentecostal preachers speaking in tongues, Indian prophets translating chicken guts to words. He gloried in the sound and in the meaning. Hoefanas and englas, sunnan and monan, steorran and earᵹan, ealle nytenu and fugelas, sae and ealle fixas God gesceop and geworhte on six dagum. He tried to show the verse to Lance, but Lance was still shouting into his cupped hands, into Toby's ear. "Relationships," he was shouting. He tried to tell Lance that these words were important, that all words were. He tried to tell him that words, even in our solitude, are magic, they make us part of something larger and better, their rhythms as well as their meaning, the way they look. He tried to say they can kill you, too, they are dangerous and animal-like, they are monstrous and deceptive and godly, they fall from copper balloons, heofanas and englas, the heavens and the angels, the sun and the moon, the stars and the earth, all beasts and birds and fish God created, and it happened in six days. Lance shouted, "She says relationships, but I know she means fucking." Toby was glad his own words were not getting through to Lance, that he was not being heard. Everything he tried to say sounded stupid and untrue. Nothing came out with the same meaning it had had in his brain. He tried to tear the page out and let Lance read it for himself. It tore across the center. He tried to tear out the other half and show them both to him. It was no use. He thought of raccoon tracks in river sand, minnows in the stream. "It's a sick world," Toby cried out. He was crying now, too. "It's not your fault," he said. "It's a bad, sick world." He stood weeping in the corner. The machines made gold-colored screws, shavings piled up on the floor.

Then, it ended. After a long time, it was over. Toby was finished crying. Lance was gone. A boy with a sawdust bucket scattered sweet-scented stuff on the oily floor and emptied the bins. Toby dried his eyes on his sleeves and blew his nose with a handkerchief. He wondered who had seen them. The Indian girl across the aisle gave no sign of having noticed. It was hard to imagine that he had been so distraught, that he could have been trapped like that. It was impossible not to wonder what was wrong with him. His body ached. He listened to the sound of the machinery.

Two of the screw machines had needed a rod for a good while now, but no damage was done. In a few minutes, the screws were filling the bins again. Toby looked at the torn page of his new book. Why on earth had he done that? He hated doing things like that; he would never get a full refund now. His head was aching badly. For a minute he thought he might cut the pages out with a razor, very neatly, and not mention it when he sent the book back to the company. No, he wouldn't do that. He didn't know what he would do. He was very tired. He signaled the foreman and went to the infirmary for aspirin.

Later, at lunch, an attractive woman came to his table and sat across from him. He recognized her as Lance Eisen's wife, who worked in Paint. She had dark blonde hair and wore makeup to cover a few acne scars on her forehead and cheeks. For a moment they said nothing. Then she said, "I think it's funny." Her voice was bitter and hurt. "I think that is just so funny." Toby McNaughton put down his sandwich and tried to think of something to say. She said, "So you think I'm sick, do you? Well, I think that is just so funny." He couldn't imagine what Lance had told her. She got up and left the table, crying.

Later still, Toby would learn that the Eisens had punched out early that day and gone home. The next day, Toby would miss work, with a high fever—a virus, the doctor would say, and in another day it would be gone. The day after that, at work, Lance Eisen would not look at him or speak to him. In two more days, Mrs. Eisen—whose name, Toby would learn, was Marilyn—would come to work with a black eye and a swollen lip. She would not be wearing her wedding ring. In weeks to come, Lance would tell Toby that he was embarrassed at what he had said and that he hoped Toby would not repeat any of it. Toby would promise, but within a few days he would have told his wife and several other persons, some of them at the plant. Soon after that, Marilyn Eisen would come to work wearing her wedding ring again, and not too long afterward, would tell her best friends that she was pregnant. Toby's correspondence course would finally come in the mail, the right one this time, and no charge would be made for the damaged book. For a while Toby would enjoy "Business Finance" and would turn in his assignments regularly. Then, finally, the math would come to seem boring and pointless. After completing about half the course, he would put it aside and, finally, forget it. Lance would be invited to help out temporarily in Engineering and, before the end of the year, would be working on a new patent with one of the real engineers, a man who said Lance could have a real future with the company.

At first Toby would feel some jealousy, but later he would forget about that, too. The day of the incident with Lance, he would go home, his head splitting, and he would drink too much and wonder that he had ever married so young and fathered a child, and although he would be too drunk to make successful love to his wife, on this day and on other days also, they would pledge their love and fall asleep in one another's arms and wake up with throbbing heads and sour breath. Late in squirrel season, he would go out into the deep woods, when the leaves were gone from the trees and the river was swift, and he would clear a spot on the foundation of the old mill and he would write his name there with a can of spray paint, the first graffiti in this part of the Ozark wilderness. The next winter he would go back and find other names and empty beer cans. That spring, China would invade Viet Nam, and Uganda would fall, and in the next county an old man in a mobile home would die in a tornado. In the same season, he would engage, for the first time, in intercourse with the Indian girl. He would tell her he loved her. He would separate from his wife and son, and he would find out, soon after, that nineteen-year-old women are fickle children. All this would happen later. But now, in the break room, at the table where he sat alone, he was almost peaceful. He finished his sandwich and put in his ear plugs and went back to Screw Machine. He fed in the rods, and the noise began and, even with the headache, he was happy. He could hear nothing, no voices, no strange words or thoughts from a book, no shouts, dangerous and appealing, no cries from the gondola, no beckoning or warning from the copper balloons, and nothing on earth, or outside it, seemed special this day to Toby McNaughton.

ONE-MAN BAND

The preacher told his daddy he would see him again next week if he could get into town. He had a wake to go to today, Rhema Fritz was dead. The old man could not speak at all since his stroke, so the preacher expected no answer and received none.

His mother was there, too. She got off her Exercycle and noted the miles on the speedometer. At the door, the preacher asked if she would like to drive out to Line Creek with him. She declined, as she did all invitations to go out, even to funerals. Before he drove off, she said, "A wake is a lonely place for a preacher, son."

The wasps were droning in the persimmon trees. The preacher—his name was Jewel Pilkington—parked his pickup and told his birddog June to stay in the bed, he didn't know how long he would be.

He spoke to the family of the dead woman. Nell was there, from Jackson, with a new permanent and frost. Myrtis was there, wearing pointy-framed bifocals. Lawrence and Gloria and others were there, too, members of Brother Pilkington's Line Creek congregation. Lela came out of the kitchen drying her hands and scratching her nose with her forearm. She asked Brother Pilkington had he had a chance to speak to Hot. "He's out back somewhere," she said, "deviling the children. Old as dirt and rich enough to burn a wet bull and all he can think to do is devil a bunch of children." Marcus was there, too, from Louisiana. Gresham hadn't been able to get away from his mission work in Mexico, but somebody said he called a while ago and sounded real good.

"In the midst of life," the preacher said, "we are in death. As for a man, his days are as the grass. But the mercy of the Lord is from everlasting to everlasting, and his righteousness unto his children's children, A-men."

He offered a prayer of thanks for Aunt Rhema's long life and fruitful issue, for her faith and strength and beauty. He was grateful, he said, for the grace of the Lord and the hope of glory and the promise of the life everlasting. This phrase caused him to remember, for some reason, a flying rooster his father had kept in their yard when Jewel was a boy, nearly forty years ago.

He had entered Aunt Rhema's house through a side door and made his way through the bedroom and the kitchen and a sleeping porch, speaking to family. In the living room, Leda Jane Fritz sat alone, weeping. She was a fashionable young woman, home from college in New York. The living room was rarely used, and the couch where she sat was protected by a clear plastic "dust cover." The preacher remembered Leda Jane as a child in his choir. He thought better of speaking to her just now. It is a rare occurrence, he reflected, unable to keep the rhythm of his preacherly voice out of even his silent thoughts, that a college girl wearing velour slacks, no brassiere, two gold chains around her neck, and yellow sunbursts on the ankles of her boots is given benefit from a Southern preacher's voice.

He moved silently through the room. He picked up a couple of doo-dads from the mantle and looked at them. One was a china cup with no handle and a deep saucer. On the white background of the cup and saucer was painted a country scene in a dark, eerie color of red. It was unlike any other the preacher had ever seen. There were tall, foreign-looking houses, all in red, with dark, red-shingled roofs. There were spires and cupolas and prominent window seats. There were odd, red trees growing along a red river, and around the borders of the scene were irrelevant red baskets of red roses. The scene gave him a queer feeling, unearthly. He looked at Leda Jane and saw that she was scarcely aware of his presence.

He looked at the scene again. He tried to imagine living in one of the red houses and dropping a hook into the red river, catching the unearthly fish that swam beneath its surface. He looked into the yards in the scene to see whether there were red people in red clothes. There were none. Then, as if it had not been there before, he saw a small red chicken. He looked twice to be sure it was really there. He searched the other yards but could find no other chickens. He set the saucer back on the mantle and picked up the cup, which was painted with the same design. There was no chicken in the yard on the cup. The painter had forgotten to put a chicken there. It was like seeing into another world. He took up the saucer again and stared deeply into the yard. There it was, the red chicken in the red yard: there and nowhere else in the world. He looked at Leda Jane and knew he had been in the room a long time without speaking, or without her speaking to him. He tried to catch her eye, but she would not look. He looked again at the saucer and remembered two things.

One was the flying rooster from his childhood. On the ground the bird seemed gray in color, but in flight an eccentric and vivid cast of red shone in all its feathers.

The other memory was of his father. Not the silent, faded ghost in the apartment, but the quiet man of Jewel Pilkington's childhood. Even then he rarely spoke, as if he were preparing for the enforced silence of his old age. Even then he shied away from telephones; he never wrote a letter. When he wanted a second helping of food, he would stop eating and stare at the dish until someone noticed and passed it to him. "The butterbeans, Daddy?" Jewel's brother Sam might say, "The okra?" Their mother would be lifting this bowl and that, hoping to hit upon the right one. "The cornbread?"

Leda Jane was still crying, noiseless. He was able to catch her

eye for a moment. When he did, she picked up a magazine and
started thumbing through it. He took the saucer with him from
the mantle and sat beside her on the couch. She shifted her body
and turned so that they would not have to speak.

He gazed back into the red scene on the saucer. He imagined
he was looking into the world of his childhood. It was September,
late afternoon and hot. Jewel was frightened of the rooster. He
stood outside the chickenyard fence beside an open spigot and
considered a drink of water. He watched his father's car pull into
the drive, a green Dodge with racks on top and two paint-stained
ladders lashed to the racks. Just then the rooster took flight.

In the western light of the Mississippi afternoon, the bird rose
from the ground—this was the first time he had seen it fly—no
longer gray, but suddenly the color of blood. There was nothing
graceful about the rooster, there was a monstrous absurdity,
frightening and comic, a pinwheel of activity, like a cartoon of a
fistfight, a whirl, blur, fists, and elbows and kneecaps sticking out
in all directions, a hand at a throat, both cartoon and a creature
of nature, soaring, large as a turkey and ungainly as an Irish setter
and, in flight, resembling both. It flew not just with wings but
with all its parts, feet and head and neck and tail and parts no man
ever saw on a chicken, arms and sails and pogo sticks, paddle-
wheels and steam whistles and circus tents with banners whipping
in the breeze, the work of God gone mad, freakshow in sunset,
stasis, confusion, and locomotion in a single beast. It covered a
distance of twenty feet and stopped outside the chickenyard. His
father turned and went into the house without speaking.

Brother Pilkington placed the saucer on an end table and decided something had to be done about Leda Jane. He placed his
hand on her shoulder. He had not noticed before what a country-
boy hand it was, the big fingers and hard nails. The hand made
his voice sound monstrous. "Job said, 'Naked came I out of my
mother's womb and naked shall I return, the Lord gave and the
Lord hath taken away, blessed be the name of the Lord.'" She
looked at him directly for the first time.

"We're all just so gamestuck, though," she said, through her earnest tears. "Not you, or Aunt Rhema, and all. Just everybody, though. Just so completely gamestuck."

The tempo of the wake was picking up now. A good deal of food had been brought in—a custom left over from a time when Mississippians would not cook in a house where a corpse lay—and a great many people had come. There was the usual amount of low talk and hugs and expressions of sympathy. The food was spread along counters and tables in the kitchen, and on the stove top and oven door. There were plates of chicken and ham. There were dishes of vegetables, a mess of greens and a skillet of cornbread, many desserts.

Miss Hunter was there, who had taught Jewel Pilkington third grade, old as ever and a little blinder. Allie Jean Scott was there, calling herself Lucinda now. Allie Jean and Jewel had started first grade together, and he could still remember her book number. "Do, Allie Jean," he said, right to her. She didn't look at him. He was no good with names.

Kimble Gregg shook the preacher's hand and thanked him for being with Aunt Rhema's people in their time of need. "I could have used you myself a time back," he said, "but I was out of state then. I guess you heard." Kimble explained that his older son, Talmedge, was killed in a plane wreck in northern Florida. Brother Pilkington said he was sorry he hadn't heard. "We're beginning to pull through," Kimble told him.

The preacher said, "He will make us strong in the hour of adversity."

"Aw, yeah," Kimble said. He put his hands into the pockets of his suit coat. After a while, he said, "Talmedge was hauling six tons of marijuana from the Keys when his plane went down. Treasury asked a bunch of questions, but they didn't make no arrests."

The house continued to fill, the talk became louder and less restrained. Brother Pilkington wondered whether now weren't maybe the time to slip out.

He eased through the living room, then stepped into a corner bedroom to get away for a minute or two. A breeze had come up and was blowing the gauzy curtains out like balloons. He gathered one side of the curtain in his hand and looked out at his truck. He knew when he parked there he was going to get blocked in. Over to one side, among the parked cars, a half dozen men were having a nip from a bottle they were passing around. He also noticed that the birddog was not in the back of the pickup. A wake is just the place for an old dog to get run over, too, he thought. Then, Brother Pilkington heard crying. Most of the crying should have been over by now.

He stepped out of the bedroom into the living room to see who it might be. The minute he was out the door, the sound was gone. He looked at the people holding plates on their laps. No one seemed to have been crying recently. He stepped back into the bedroom.

There it was again, the sound of crying. It had a desperate sound, and it worried him. Then he understood. Someone was in the pantry, just on the other side of the closet wall. He made his way through the house and found the pantry door.

He stepped inside and eased the door shut behind him. It was Woodrow Fritz, a child of sixteen, too old to be out playing with the other children, the youngest of the adults. Woodrow's daddy had talked to the preacher about him before. "He's big as a walrus," the man had said, "you can see that yourself, and real morbid for his age." Woodrow was a big boy, there was no denying that, but not big like a walrus. He was big like a man of thirty. At least six inches taller than the preacher, six foot four probably, with long, dark hair on his forearms. He was weeping uncontrollably over the death of Aunt Rhema. The light had not been on, so the preacher reached up and felt for the string.

The light startled the boy. "Don't you come in here with that damn sanctimonious voice of yours, preacher," he said. "Ain't nothing going to keep old man Morocco from pickling Aunt

Rhema, so just keep that goddamn self-righteous voice of yours
to yourself. Ain't nothing going to keep me from being mad
about it."

Brother Pilkington would have liked to oblige, but it was the
only voice that would come to him. "Anger is no sin," he said, "it
is a cleansing. Even our Lord and King felt anger."

It infuriated the boy. He strained his neck muscles, tears flowed
from his eyes. Worse, he was pacing around the room, slamming
his fist into his hand. He wanted something to hit.

The bulb and cord swayed back and forth. The light caused
strange shadows to fall around the little room. Mason jars wavered
in the light, sliced pears in syrup, glistening red plums. Light
caught and released the bottles, clingstone peaches, with their
blood-red centers and orange meat, pickled okras, animallike in
the vinegar and dill, cucumbers and green tomatoes, row after row
of Blue Lake green beans, dewberry preserves and whole figs.
They moved with the bulb and cord. The boy's grief threatened
to turn to violence.

Brother Pilkington thought of Aunt Rhema as the boy might
be remembering her, solitary old woman picking fruit along a
ditchbank, beneath the Petticocowa bridge, or by the cow pond,
wondering as she picked whether the winter would be cold enough
to kill the duckweed on the water. He imagined her, as he had
seen her, with a bandana tied around her neck, her unlaced brogans
flopping on her feet beneath a fig tree. She reached up and felt the
ooze of fig milk on her rough fingers. He imagined those same
fingers rubbed over the smooth-skinned plums, the lean, wiry old
woman, whose death this child grieved without understanding
grief. She stood with uplifted arms among the fruit trees, as if she
were a tree herself, growing up out of the Johnson grass and lespedeza, arms upstretched like branches.

"I'll tell you what," the boy said, with decision in his voice,
"I'll tell you. I'm going to break every goddamn jar in this pantry."

Woodrow grabbed one of the jars of green beans and turned
as if he might actually hit the preacher with it. It was not a thing
he was incapable of. When his mother lost a child a year ago, a

premature birth that lived only seven hours, Woodrow brooded and wept and, finally, threw a double-bladed ax through the window of his father's pickup. Only luck prevented someone's being in the truck at the time.

"Woody, for God's sake, man," the preacher said.

"I'll bust your goddamn face."

"Woodrow, the time is at hand. Seize it." Brother Pilkington was not sure what he meant by this, but it affected the boy. It seemed right, psalmic and magical and wise, in his preacherly voice.

"I can just see her, though," Woodrow said. He held the quart jar behind his head, and the preacher knew he might still throw it, but his voice had already begun to lose the anger, to take a tone of despair and pleading. "I can just see her, out by the chickenhouse, and it getting dark and the air so cool and no sound except the cluck-cluck-cluck and her going 'Chick, oh chick-chick,' in her little old-woman voice, like nobody's listening, not even the chickens, just talking to herself and scattering shelled corn, you know, and maybe an owl just starting to hoot or that sound the big plums make when they fall off the tree and hit the grass out by the fence, and all the shadows, and when it's over, putting her old skinny hand back on her neck where it's aching and then knocking the dishpan against her leg to shake out the corn dust."

So, it was over. Woodrow put the jar of green beans back on the shelf and took the handkerchief the preacher handed him. It was the same one Leda Jane had used, but he didn't notice. He looked like a giant, and his great arms hung down.

"Woodrow," the preacher said, when some time had passed. "Son, do you know what is going to happen to you the next time you speak either directly or indirectly of the sanctimony you say you find in my speaking voice?"

The huge boy said, "Yessir."

"I'm going to whip your ass like you got caught stealing chickens, ain't I?"

"Yessir," he said.

The sun was a good deal declined and had lost its ardent interest
in the pastures and fields and ponds and sheds. The shadows of
the house and trees fell across one side of the yard and made a
pleasant shade.

Funeral guests had been leaving for a while now, and others
were starting up their pickups and station wagons and cars. Breeze
from the back pastures, where Brother Pilkington could still hear
children playing, brought a fresh smell of hay and manure and
fishy pond water to his nostrils. He was tired.

The men were finished drinking whiskey. They sat around the
backyard, a few on the porch steps, others in chairs they had
brought out. A cow with a bell walked toward the shed.

Brother Pilkington stepped out onto the porch and found an
empty spot on the steps. He hiked up his pants legs above his socks
and sat slowly. Yellow and pink were already smeared through
the clouds in the south and west. June, the preacher's dog, with
cockleburrs in her ears, eased into the company of men and took
her place beside the preacher. "Old liver-spot," he said.

In a little while, the men were talking in quiet voices, telling
stories. The women were mostly inside, talking about Lord knew
what. Everybody was gone now except family and a few close
neighbors. One man asked did they remember back when Line
Creek used to flood. "Back before they built the levees on the
Yazoo and Tallahatchie," he said. "The water used to come up past
the road and get in the hen houses. If you weren't careful, it would
drown the chickens and the eggs would float off and rot. Children
would paddle out in wood boats and gather rotten eggs to throw
at one another. Miss Bartlin had a cow drown one time. There
was cholera somewhere or other, not right around Line Creek, out
in Carroll County, maybe, or down to Morgan City. All the dead
livestock had to be burned, didn't matter what they died of, even
drowning. She burned that cow for a month, seem like, before
it would ever burn up. Just keep on throwing stove wood and coal
oil on it. And stunk, godamighty. Just keep on burning it, night
and day, and the colored folks all down Line Creek keeping an eye

out, trying to see can they pick up sight of a cross in the middle
of all that burning. And then even them able to forget about it.
Truckers and travelers—I used to think about this all the time when
I was a boy—folks driving out on Highway 49, seven eight miles
away, could see the smoke, that old greasy black smoke, and
they'd say, 'There's the Line Creek community, Miss Bartlin still
burning that cow,' and Miss Bartlin real mad at Lonnie Weber,
used to be town marshal—he's the one made her burn it, said he
was under orders from the Public Health, and her not saying
nothing except how she's just a pore woman and can't afford to
burn no cow. Law," he said. He slowed down the pace of his tale
to signal the end. "Law, them was funny times, long time ago.
Funny times."

For a while nothing was said. Then the man who had been
talking said, "Which, I don't know if you know it, is where that
expression come from, when you say a man is rich enough to burn
a wet bull. And stunk, godamighty."

The colors in the sky were more vivid now against the clouds.
The cow whose bell the preacher had heard had made its way
up the pasture to the feed trough and was switching horseflies with
its tail. A couple of egrets, solemn birds far from their homes in
the cypress trees on Roebuck Lake, stood around the feed lot
looking at the cows.

The preacher stood up and stretched. It was late, he said. About
time for him and old June to be moving toward home. He still
had his horse yet to feed. The other men began to stand up too and
agree that it was late. They shook the preacher's hand. Somebody
kicked the cat off the porch to stretch his legs.

Inside, he said his goodbyes to the women. Some shook his
hand, others gave him a hug and thanked him. Woodrow Fritz
avoided his eye, but Leda Jane followed him out to his truck and
told him she would be heading back to New York soon after the
funeral. If she didn't get to talk to him later, she just, well, wanted

to say goodbye. Brother Pilkington was too tired to figure out
what she was trying to tell him.

He helped June into the bed of the pickup and noticed that she
was more feeble this year than last. He slammed the door and said,
"Now don't you forget us up there in the big city, Miss Leda."
He started the engine and began backing out of the drive. He could
hear Uncle Hot, herding up the children with promises of sweet
things to eat.

He had started to tell the men in the back yard about his father,
the story of the flying rooster. He could have made them laugh.
Or he could have been serious. He could have told them the rooster was an emblem of Aunt Rhema's soul's ascension, released at
last from the clay, speeding heavenward, monstrous and swift and
absurd, without grace or beauty but confident and purposeful,
hightailing it for a neighbor's chickenyard or the streets of gold.
He might have told them he worried about his father and mother,
and wondered that their lives could have come to so little. He
might have said that when he tried to understand, he could remember only the rooster. When he sees, in his memory, the rooster
in flight, he sees also a world of bright skies and pungent catalpa
beans and honey in the comb, he sees planets and suns and galaxies
infinitely deep and beautiful, and he hears music. He believes
every image and every song come from his sad mother and father,
a tale of growth and death and resurrection, of irrevocable loss
and unexpected joy in the hope of renewal.

It was just as well he had not told them. He switched on the
headlights and headed out the gravel road towards the parsonage.

By the time he pulled his pickup around behind the house,
the sky was dark. There was a moon, though. He fed his horse
and stood beside it in the dark for a while as it ate, then he opened
the shed door for it to go in.

The porchlight was not on, but he could see. He stamped his
feet on the board floor of the porch and went into the house by
the kitchen door. He had not known just how tired he was. He
struck a match and lit the oven to take the chill out of the room.

He sat heavily in a chair at the kitchen table and stretched out his legs and closed his eyes. He wondered how much longer they could keep his daddy at home. For a while he thought nothing else, he just sat. He may have slept for a minute.

When he opened his eyes, he felt better, less tired. Still, he didn't get up yet. The table where he sat was made of wood, with a square of oilcloth to cover it. He drummed his fingers against the table top, slowly at first, and the rhythm pleased him. He stopped and let his hand rest, palm down, on the oilcloth. He started again, drumming his fingers and listening to the sound.

He drummed harder, and a little faster, and he kept on drumming. He wondered where the rhythm was coming from, what part of his mind had invented the rhythm his fingers made. He listened inside his head, and he drummed what he heard. He kept on drumming. For emphasis he struck the table extra hard with his index finger, and sometimes with his thumb; for a different sound he angled his fingers so that his nails hit first and then the blunt tips of flesh and bone. He listened in his head and he kept on drumming, imitating the sounds that he heard. He loved the sound, he had heard it somewhere before. Now he used the heel of his hand sometimes, and sometimes he would slap the table with his palm, a-rat-a-tat-tat and a boom slap crack, and the drumming went on, hard fingers and hard nails and a country-boy hand going bang-bang-bump. And he bumped and he banged and he listened to the Psalms and he looked down from heaven on the children of men, and he wished he had married and fathered a son, and he missed his brother Sam who lived on the Gulf, and he thought about his mama and he grunted and he whistled and he clicked with his tongue, Hambone. Hambone, Hambone, have you heard, Papa's gonna buy me a mockingbird. He sang out loud to the yellow walls, he breathed the heated air from the open oven door, he wanted Leda Jane, he wanted her in his bed, Hambone. He slapped with his hand from his leg to his chest, from his chest to his leg, and he made a loud pop on his open-oh mouth, and he ached for his daddy and the rooster and for death, and he sang to his mama of a one-man band, oh he sang of a one-man band.

SUGAR AMONG
THE FREAKS

I knew I had made a mistake when the iced tea came with a spoon sticking out of it. I was in the Skelly truck-stop restaurant in Alma, Arkansas. It's got a sign that says Home Cooking and a glass case full of slabs of coconut pie and chocolate pie with real dilapidated meringue on them and a couple of flies crawling around on the inside of the glass.

Meringue and flies don't mean a thing compared to tea. You can scoop that meringue off and sling it up under some furniture and never see it again, and there's not a nickel's worth of taste in a fly, even if you do happen to eat one. It's the iced tea in a place that predicts what the food is going to look like when it comes out. I learned that from my mama, who served instant potato sandwiches on light bread. She also pronounced meringue as merry-gew, if you want some idea of what kind of cook she was.

In fact, I've got to tell you about my mama. She used to cut a magnolia blossom off the tree in our side yard and put it on the dining room table for decoration. "Big as a dinner plate," she would always say, which made it sound kind of sickening in the first place, if you see what I mean. It was so sweet-smelling it would give you cavities. Not really, of course. That was my grandmama's joke, Sugar Mecklin. I wanted to live with Sugar, but nobody would let me. The magnolia wouldn't cause cavities, but it would give you Excedrin Headache Number 57, if you remember your t.v. commercials at all, before you could jerk a cat in two. That's the one where two ram goats are butting each other in the head.

The worst thing was she would leave it on the table so long. She would leave it there a month, seem like. She would leave it there until it was all black and horrible and runny before she would throw it out. Even if she'd been a better cook you couldn't have eaten in the presence of that magnolia. Nobody could. My daddy could, of course. But not any normal person, no way, José, which is something else my Grandmama Sugar used to say.

I took one look at that tea and I said, "Instant!" right out loud, couldn't have stopped myself if I tried. Some customers looked over at me. I said "Instant" another couple of times real loud, and clapped my hands together when I said it. They might think *instant* means waitress in German or some other language, you don't know. Some people will believe anything.

You're going to say, "Now he sounds a little crazy to me," and I don't blame you a bit. I am crazy, I act that way. I start acting crazy whenever I'm under the influence of Winston Krepps.

Winston is this guy I help out whenever he asks me. He's a full-time quadriplegic, got him a motorized wheelchair and everything. I was supposed to meet Winston at this truck stop and help his attendant drive him out to west Oklahoma to some kind of conference he was going to.

Winston jumped off a bridge when he was a boy and hit a submerged boat, broke his neck pretty as you please. I said, "I bet you won't be jumping off any more bridges any time soon, will you," and Winston said he had to agree. He said he learned his lesson the first time. I lived with Winston for a while a couple years ago, helped him out. He says I ought to get a more realistic view of life, and other helpful advice. I have to agree.

I get along fine with Winston. The trouble is, I've got this personality flaw. That's what Winston told me. I'm ashamed to tell you about it, but here's the truth. Deformed people make me go crazy. You're going to say, "Uh-oh, look out, he's a mean one."

It's not true. Winston'll tell you that himself. I'm as sweet a guy as you ever want to meet—Sugar Mecklin, named after my grand-mama. Twenty-four years old, high school equivalency diploma— I mean what else do you want, Burt Reynolds, or what?

But I never can treat deformed people or crippled people like they're real. To me they're just a bunch of freaks, not much better than a midget. And don't get me started on the blind. I took work out at the School for the Blind in Little Rock for a while, so I know what's on a blind man's mind. They've got this good sense of smell, though, I'll give them that.

Anyway, it's a problem I've got. Winston says it doesn't matter to him; he likes me anyway, which I appreciate. Oh, I get along fine with Winston. I wouldn't go so far as to say I like him. No sense lying about that. You can't go around having a passel of freaks as your friends. No way, José.

Part of it is I run into so many of them. In the Safeway, squeezing cantelopes, look out!—somebody's going to sneak up behind you and hand you a deaf-mute card and cost you a quarter and make you think for about the one millionth time that you might try to learn sign language off the hand illustrations on the back.

Or you're down at Roger's Ozark Pool Hall, shooting a little snooker, hold on!—here comes a man with one leg shorter than the other, and he's wearing one of those built-up shoes, rocking his way around the table, rocka rocka rocka, while he chalks his cue and takes you for every nickel you got in your pocket. How are you going to shoot snooker with a rocker?

I went out with a girl one time who showed me a glass eye she wore around her neck on a gold chain. I never asked her whose eye it was, I just drove her home. I counted myself lucky I hadn't made a big hit with her. Think about taking a girl's blouse off and finding an eye staring out at you. What kind of life can you live when you keep meeting people who might do that to you.

And you try applying for a job in Fort Smith, second largest town in Arkansas. Just try it and see what happens. A third of the men you shake hands with will have two fingers missing on their right hand, and the rest of them will be wearing a hearing aid. They wear those flesh-colored rascals that fit behind your ear and look like you've got a disease. I can't stand a hearing aid. One of those big curved horns you used to see in pictures would be all right, but not something that looks like ear disease.

Deformed people are attracted to me, see. I'm a lightning rod and they're a big dark cloud just rubbing his old hands together he's so happy.

Wait till I tell you what happened to me when I was a child growing up in Mississippi. A pipeline for natural gas was being put through the Delta and had everybody all excited. A lot of new work opened up. Transient workers from all over the country piled into our little town in trailers. My daddy, trying to latch onto some of the new money that was flowing through, rented out our side yard with the magnolia tree. It was a good place for a mobile home hook-up, he said. You probably already know what happened. A family of midgets moved in. You wouldn't think there would be many midgets in the construction field, would you? But there they were, a whole trailerful of them.

I used to be Winston's attendant. That's the kind of job I'm always getting myself into. I lived with him for about six months before he moved to Hot Springs to teach in the Rehab Center there. He's a poet, and they tell me he understands the problems of the handicapped and is well appreciated for his good work. I don't doubt it a bit.

Here's the thing, though. It was a relief to me when he moved down there. When I was living with him I had this unhealthy compulsion to be the best attendant the world has ever known. Winston says I ought to try to break myself of that. He says I'm just a generous kind of guy and I take everything too far, even generosity.

I didn't catch on to what I was doing at the time, but I think I see it now. I would do anything in the world that Winston told me, and I mean anything. My goal was to give Winston the freedom to do anything he would have done if he never had jumped off that bridge in the first place.

He said, "Okay, what if I told you I couldn't stand you? What if I said I'd shoot you dead if I could hold a gun and pull the trigger?" I swear, it scared me. I didn't know the answer. I knew it wouldn't come to that. Winston wouldn't do that to me. But you see what I mean. It's a question you want to know the answer to.

I did plenty of other stuff though. If Winston was dead drunk and wanted more whiskey, I poured it down him, brother, no questions asked, forget about tomorrow. Next day he'd be sick and I'd be holding the pan he was gagging into and he'd catch his breath for a second and he'd say, "Use your goddamn brain, man! Don't feed a drunk man whiskey!" Too late, and just don't tell me to do it again, we'll both be smelling vomit in the morning. That's what I would think; I wouldn't say it. I make it a rule never to disagree with a freak.

If he wanted to blow the horn in traffic, I blew it, forget about rude, forget about unnecessary. If Winston wanted to stay late at a party that everybody else had already left and the host wanted us the hell out of his house, we stayed. "Christ, don't let me do that again," he'd say when he caught on to what had happened. Same thing—don't ask it again. Plenty of times I drove down roads I knew were the wrong road, because Winston had misread the map. I made wrong turns into one-way traffic, because Winston had his directions mixed up.

I understand it better now. Winston explained it to me. He said it was a way of redressing the wrong in myself, what I knew was wrong. He said I felt guilty for thinking he wasn't real. He said I was trying to act like he, Winston, was the real person and that I was the one that was something else, something less. He said it would suit him fine if I was to disagree with him sometime. He said it would beat hell out of driving into one-way traffic.

It didn't help. I still do whatever a freak tells me. When I'm under the influence of Winston, even nonfreaks can control me.

Like the tea, for example. I can't stand instant tea. My mama, who was the worst cook you ever want to meet up with, used to make instant tea when I was little. They say the product has been improved since then but it's a lie, it's the same.

My mama wasn't deformed, but she was a kind of freak. My
daddy actually called her a freak one time, right to my face. We
were sitting out on the porch swing, and Daddy was shooting out
the Christmas lights around the porch, still up in August, with a
Red Ryder bee-bee gun, manufactured at the plant right out here
in Springdale, with a leather thong hanging off the side. He said,
right out of the clear blue, like when a daddy decides his boy ought
to be told some important thing that he'll need to know about for
the rest of his life, like about tail or something, he said, "Sugar,
your mama is a first-class freak. It has not escaped my attention."
What's a child going to do with that kind of information, I ask
you? He was telling me he loved my mother. He might just as well
have said, "I have been cursed with premature ejaculation, but I
love family life anyway." What's a child supposed to say? What's he
supposed to think about for the rest of his life? And anyway, who
arranged for the midgets to live in the side yard with the magnolia
tree? Not Mama. I remember she did introduce me to a clubfooted
Latvian girl, and she kept giving us that look that says she's just
dying for us to like each other right away and get married and
have her a passel of little clubfooted Latvian grandchildren, but
she doesn't want to seem pushy so just go right on and take
our time.

I knew I was going to drink that tea the minute I saw it. I
caught a couple of flies with my hand, just to calm down. I took
the tea from the waitress and said, "Donkey shane, honey." I was
using my German accent to deal with her; couldn't hurt.

The reason was, this waitress had a mean look. She was old
and had heavy biceps and old-fashioned heart-shaped lips painted
over her regular lips. I didn't look to see if she had her stockings
rolled down to her ankles or was wearing white socks, but I bet it
was one or the other. She wasn't wearing any kind of waitress
uniform, just a plain blue dress with a broad collar. She looked like
somebody who was having to work on her day off, so just watch
out, Jack, don't mess with her.

I wasn't wrong about the tea. I looked down in the glass. There was a solid brown mass at the bottom. I pushed it around and around until it broke up and an amber foam floated up to the top. Presweetened and lemon flavored, same as Mama used to make, you could smell it.

And I wasn't wrong about the food either. It was as bad as Mama's. In fact, I've got to tell you about Mama's cooking. The scariest meal she fixed was spaghetti. The recipe was real simple. For the sauce she dumped a couple of quarts of canned tomatoes into a big skillet, along with an onion chopped into four pieces. That was all. There were no other ingredients. No garlic, no salt, no meat, no oregano—nothing. Listen to this. When the tomatoes were bubbling, she stripped the cellophane off a package of noodles and, without separating them, jammed them up under the hot tomatoes like a short baton. They just sat there and cooked until they were a solid gummy rod of pasta.

My daddy, he was a little red-faced man with webbed toes on both his feet and went around barefoot all the time. He claimed this was his favorite dish. He would clean his plate. I mean he really liked it, he wasn't just being nice. He'd finish up and he'd say, "Whew!" He'd push his chair back from the table and stretch out his little short legs with his old duck toes hanging off the end, and he'd pat his stomach with both hands. He'd say, "I ought not, I'm going to get fat if I do, but, honey, if you'd be kind enough to slice me off another three four inches of that spaghetti, I do believe I could find a place for it." Do you see what I mean? It's no wonder I've got some personality problems.

I played it safe with the waitress. I wrapped the Salisbury steak up in a paper napkin and stuffed it inside the torn plastic lining of the chair I was sitting in. I let the mashed potatoes get cold and stiff enough to stick to the underside of the table. I hoped they would hang there long enough for me to make my getaway. I didn't know what to do with the cole slaw, so I scooped it up in the palm of my hand and looked around the room. When I thought nobody was looking, I lobbed it onto a table nearby. Nobody was sitting at the table, and the dishes from the last customer hadn't been bused yet. I had hoped it would hit one of the plates. It didn't, but it looked okay where it did hit, mostly in one of the ashtrays.

When the waitress brought the check, she noticed I had cleaned my plate. For a second there I thought she was going to tell me what a good boy I was, but she didn't. She just gave me one of her suspicious looks and slapped the check down in front of me. I think I know why she was mad at me. I got the impression she could tell I hitchhiked in here. I got the impression she knew I had caught two rides to get here, the first one to Winslow with a college boy in a 280Z and the other one with a man in a twenty-five-year-old Cadillac. I got the impression she knew he told me he was driving to Waco to kill his brother-in-law and showed me the pistol he was going to use. I got the impression she was thinking, You're batting .500 already, sonnyboy, don't try nothing smart with me. I got the impression hitchhikers are on an especially low rung of the social ladder in a truck stop, especially those who can't do any better than an Arky college boy and a murderous Texan. She didn't say a word about it, but I've got this ability.

Just then Winston and his attendant drove up. The attendant's name was Floyd, Winston had told me on the phone. I recognized the van right away, when I saw it out the window. It's a white Ford with a hydraulic lift on the back. I thought about Winston and remembered he would be in his old heavy humming buzzing chair. I couldn't stand that thing.

Old Biceps looked in my direction from the next table. She had found the ashtray full of cole slaw and didn't act happy about it. I checked the mashed potatoes and thought they had started to lose their grip.

I eased away from the table and went outside in the parking lot to meet Winston and Floyd. I didn't know Floyd, just his name, which sounded a little sissified to me, if you want the truth. The waitress was still busy with the slaw problem and didn't see me leave.

Now here is the way things can turn on you. I had been worrying

about dealing with Winston being a freak. There was a bigger
problem with Floyd. He wasn't the pretty-boy I had expected. In
fact, he was extra ugly. He was ugly enough to qualify for a full-
time freak, if you ask me. Sugar Mecklin would have said he was
ugly enough to strike you blind. I shook hands with him out in
the parking lot and went blind.

It's the truth, I couldn't see him. The only thing I noticed about
him before I lost my sight was that Floyd was a black man. I
wouldn't want you to think I'm prejudiced against black people.
You might think so, since you know I grew up in Mississippi. But
it's not true. In fact, I grew up thinking my family was part Ne-
gro. My Grandmama Sugar told me ever since I can remember
that she was one-quarter black. She'd say, "One-quarter black,
and it had to be the hind quarter."

Her right leg and hip weren't black exactly, they were more
purple. It was a birthmark, I guess. I don't know what age I was
before I finally caught on that she was making a joke. I used to
roll around on the linoleum floor of her kitchen and try to look up
Sugar's dress to see how high her blackness went. She'd kick me
away from the sink, real playful, and she'd say, "You little freak."

Anyway, Floyd was black and I couldn't see him. I looked, but
he just wasn't there. It turned out, though, that I wasn't blind
after all. Floyd was invisible. I could see everything around him. I
saw the parked tractor trailers, I saw the greasy asphalt and the
diesel pumps. I could see Winston just fine. He looked all right,
too, as good as he ever looks. But Floyd wasn't there. He was too
ugly to be seen.

Winston said that before he ate he wanted to be taken into the
souvenir section of the truck stop. He said he was collecting ma-
terial for a poem. I knew what he wanted to look at. He wanted
to look at the Bowie knives and billy clubs and Confederate flags
and bumper plates that say I Just Barfed and I'm Glad and oil
paintings of Jesus riding shotgun in a Kenworth hauling logs.

Floyd said, "Nah, we don't have time."

Do you think I'd ever say such a thing to Winston?

Winston said, "I'm going in there, open the door."

Floyd wouldn't do it. Floyd said, "What you want me to get you to eat?"

Winston dropped the subject of the souvenirs and rolled into the restaurant. He said, "I believe I'll have a beer."

Floyd said, "You don't want any beer."

I thought, I like Floyd pretty good, invisible or not. It was an odd thing to be thinking, if you see what I mean.

All during the meal I spoke with this exaggerated British accent. It tickled Winston and Floyd to death, but I was serious. You can't go into a restaurant with a pair of freaks and not do something to protect yourself. I used words like *bloody good* and *old chap* and *amusing*. Partly it was to throw the waitress off my trail. We had Lady Biceps again, and I didn't know whether she had found the Salisbury steak or not.

The funny part is, she didn't recognize me. I'm terrible with accents, and I never fool anybody, but with her it was working perfect. She looked at me like I wasn't there at all. She could see Floyd just fine, you could tell, but she couldn't see me. It scared me a little, to tell the truth, even though I always thought it would be kind of nice to be invisible.

One time I paid a woman at a carnival five dollars to make me invisible, and do you think she would do it? Why, no. She tried to give me the five dollars back. She said I reminded her of her poor little sweet nephew who was a harelip (which I'm not) and why didn't I just run on and spend my money on something else. I said, "Uh-unh, honey, we made a deal. I got a signed contract." She said, "I ain't a real gypsy. I was just lying to you. I can't make nobody invisible. You scat." You talk about mad, that was me. I tore that contract up right in her sassy face. Her name was Sister Medium Jackson, and she could have done it too, if she'd tried.

Right now I had this waitress problem. I made some squawking and hooting noises at her, like jungle birds and monkeys. I stretched out the features of my face with my fingers. It didn't faze her a bit. She didn't bat an eye. She wasn't faking either. She didn't give me that look that says she really does see me and she knows what a bratty little jackass I am and wouldn't my mama be ashamed of me if she knew the kind of fool I'm playing in a public place but just you wait and see how long it takes her to bat an eye she doesn't care how crazy I act. That wasn't her. She really couldn't see me, just like I couldn't see Floyd. I thought invisibility wasn't all it was cracked up to be. I thought Sister Medium Jackson was a pretty nice old girl after all, back in that sawdusty old horse lot they called a carnival in Mississippi, trying to save me five dollars and a hard time.

But mostly I felt all alone and left out. I hated being invisible, even to just one person. I felt awful that I had probably made Floyd feel the same way. I looked at him again and hoped I'd be able to see him, but I couldn't. Still invisible. These are strange times we are living in, I'm telling you.

I wanted out of the Skelly station. I kept looking at the black hole of Floyd, trying to see him in there somewhere, peeking out or something. The blackness didn't have anything to do with his race. Floyd was like watching an eclipse of the moon, except there was no light around the rim. I wondered if anybody who could be invisible could be real, even myself. But that wasn't it. It wasn't a blackness of Floyd's not being there. It was like he was too much there, like a real black hole in space you hear so much about, like he's pure there, not like most everybody else, who are only half-assed here. I got the feeling Floyd's ugliness was only just the tiniest little bit of his real ugliness, like it had been distilled down to this and maybe could be bottled in a little glass decanter and sold on the open market for a million dollars an ounce for real pretty women to put behind their ears before they go out on a date to calm down some of that prettiness and get a little bit ugly like the rest of us so we won't feel uncomfortable when they come around.

I said, "I've got to get out of here. I'm going crazy."

Winston and Floyd said they had to agree.

The drive to Oklahoma was long and hard, but I didn't mind. I

was happy to be in the van, behind the wheel. Sometimes cars
would pass us, and one time a child in the backseat caught a
glimpse of Floyd and had a conniption fit and his mama and daddy
probably wondered what in the world, but mostly nobody even
looked. We drove until it got dark, and we kept on driving.

It was real late. The traffic through Oklahoma City was fierce.
Every cowboy and Indian in the state was out driving around in
pickups. We kept on going.

After a while we pulled off the road for gas. It was the middle
of the night by now, and the station we stopped at was deserted
except for us. We pulled up alongside the pumps and I saw the
station attendant come out of the little lighted office and head our
way. He was just a boy.

I could see that his name was sewn on his shirt, up over the
Exxon patch, but I didn't read it. I knew his name already. I have
this mental ability. His name would be Jimmy, and his last name
would be Fish. I looked around for his daddy, whose name would
be Ellis, then I realized his daddy wouldn't be working in a ser-
vice station. He would be assistant manager of the planing mill.

Jimmy Fish was in his late teens. He was a skinny boy with a
big adam's apple and pretty good teeth. He looked tired and
friendly. I watched him come up to the van on Floyd's side. Floyd
turned towards him, and they met face to face.

Here's the thing. One time when I was Jimmy Fish's age, I had
a temporary job in the complaint department of a big store. It was
the day after Christmas, and I was making exchanges on Christmas
presents that were being brought back. It was a pretty good job,
too, tissue paper in your hands all day and the smell of cardboard
in your nostrils. Where are you going to get a better job than that?
I was sitting framed behind an open window at a counter. I waited
on a long line of polite dissatisfied customers. Look up, smile,
inspect the merchandise, do the paper work, look up again, next
customer. Nothing to it. Then I looked up into the face of a
monster.

It was a woman with no face. There was no nose, only a wet
hole to breathe through. There were no lips, only teeth. There

was a wild caged tongue that was roaring for freedom from behind its bars. There was one eye, wide open and hairless as a fish eye. The other eye was sealed shut. There was no hair, only a badly fitted wig that couldn't hide the fact that she didn't have any ears. There were sermons that might have been preached on that good woman's suffering. No sermons came to my mind. I screamed. A loud horrible out-of-control scream.

Everybody in the line of customers hated me for noticing her deformity. The store manager sent me home. People comforted the monster, who couldn't cry because her tear glands had been blown away in the explosion along with everything else. I was not proud of that scream.

I expected Jimmy Fish to scream like that when he saw Floyd. I was wrong. Do you know what Jimmy Fish said? He said, "Unleaded?"

I wanted to be like Jimmy Fish. I wanted to be anybody but myself. I wanted to blame my crazy mama and daddy for making me so crazy. I wanted to blame Winston and Floyd. I couldn't. Blame had never seemed so out of place. I looked at Floyd and hoped I might be able to see him. I thought if I could see him I wouldn't hate myself so much.

He was still invisible, but he had changed. A dim halo had formed around his eclipsed face, his eclipsed self. I looked at Jimmy Fish. I admired him. I admired his innocence. I admired him for never having lived in Mississippi with a yardful of midgets. I admired these dark Oklahoma plains. I loved the people of this moony land. I knew that nobody in Oklahoma would ever scream into a woman's face, no matter how ugly she was.

I stopped myself. I made a couple of jungle noises, to test the air. I placed my right hand inside my shirt, in my armpit, and blew off a couple of quick bilabials. It was love. Love is what I was up against. I fought it.

I resisted the easiness of love you feel when you meet a boy in the middle of the night and you think he reminds you of yourself and yet you know he represents everything you could never have been because you had midgets and he didn't, and you were once invisible and he wasn't, and you couldn't see Floyd and had screamed in a woman's face and learned to eat spaghetti by the slice. I resisted loving anyone for the reason that he was not deformed and that his family was not crazy and that he fit, anyway, into a world of deformity better than I did.

I looked out the window on my side of the van. The boy was pumping gas. I made a sound like a siren at him, and he only looked up and smiled. He made small talk. He told me about a man he saw on Real People, the t.v. show, who called himself the Human Siren. I barked at him and snarled at him, and he started telling me the plot of a werewolf movie. I loved him, but I didn't want to love him.

I resisted love because I knew that Jimmy Fish was not the thing I loved. The love I felt had no object. It was flying loose everywhere in a whirlwind; it had no place to light. Jimmy Fish was the first scrap of bark it came to and clung to by its toenails. I remembered a time when my mama invited the midgets into our home for dinner.

She served them her unbelievable spaghetti. The midgets thought a cruel joke was being played on them. The father of the little family took a deep breath. He got up, with dignity, from his chair. He jerked the napkin back through the napkin ring and put it beside his plate. He said, "We will go now. I understand now." With his tiny wife and three midget children squeaking and peeping and cheeping behind him, he made his lofty exit and never entered our home again.

I was a child at that table. I felt as embarrassed and as alone and as different as the midgets. I ran out of the house by the back door. I hid in the ditch under the chinaberry tree and watched them. I dreamed of finding words to apologize to them. I never did. I could never bring myself to speak to any of them again.

When the pipeline was finished and they moved out of our yard, I was the loneliest person in the world. I felt like a child who dies before it gets baptized, like somebody told me, and has to wander around all through eternity by himself and so lonesome

he can't stand it. I was on a journey too, always had been, and I'm
not off it yet, maybe never will be. Winston told me the kind of
journey it is. He said I was on a Journey Through the Land of the
Flat Characters. I know what he means now. It means that all my
life I've been on an excursion through hell, and at every gate a new
freak is crouched to jump out at me and scare me and refuse to
let me get back up to the light. I want to get out, but I can't find
my way.

I resisted love, I clawed at it, I scratched it with my fingernails.
I bit off its nose. But it was still there. It was love, and it was real.
When Jimmy Fish did not scream, love swept through me like a
sudden wind. I felt it. It felt like the breeze made by the wings of
a million bats swarming up out of a cave, squealing. I thought I
was one of the bats in the swarm. This was love to me. Behind us
a million tons of bat shit on the floor of the cave, and all around
us nothing but a blaze of starlight and a million piercing shrill cries
to be read with our pained ears like a million tiny white canes
with red tips tap-tap-tapping along a sidewalk looking for
the curb.

I was in love, but not with Jimmy or Winston or Floyd or
myself. I was in love with America. The love I felt—crazy, diffuse,
bat-out-of-hell love—was patriotism. I loved America. I loved
Exxon. I loved the Ford Motor Company, who built the van that
brought me to Oklahoma and this insight. I loved America's
golden indifference to deformity. I loved American parents, who
could name the ugliest child to be born in modern times with a
pretty-boy's name. I loved American consumers, who hated me
for screaming at a monster. I loved American politicians, who
treated Floyd to a free education at the Rehabilitation Center Trade
School for the simple reason that he was ugly as hell and had ap-
plied for a scholarship on those grounds. America the beautiful!
I almost sang it. Land of the freaks and home of the strange.

I looked at Floyd. I smiled my brightest smile into his invisibility. Out of his eclipse he said, "Are you okay, man?"

I said, "Floyd, I am proud to be an American!"

Winston looked at me, and then at Floyd. They both seemed worried about me. Winston said, "We're all tired. We're all getting punchy."

I tried to curb my enthusiasm. They were probably right. I probably did sound a little wild. I went inside the station and gave Jimmy Fish Winston's credit card.

I said, "Fine night, Jimmy, just *fine!*" Jimmy didn't say anything. I was sorry I had had to make the noises at him, happy he had not seemed to notice. I wanted to ask about Ellis, but I decided against it. Maybe people in Oklahoma aren't named Ellis. Maybe there are no planing mills in Oklahoma.

Jimmy Fish handed me the credit slip to sign. He said, "Write down your tag number."

I made up a number and wrote Arkansas in the block marked State.

He took the slip and read it over, real careful. I was afraid he would know I was lying about the license number. He didn't care about the number. He said, "Arkansas," reading from the slip. His voice didn't have much expression. He didn't hand back the credit card or my copy of the bill yet. He said, "Whereabouts in Arkansas."

I said, "Hot Springs." Not much of a lie.

He said, "My granddaddy used to live in Arkansas."

I said, "Is that right."

He said, "Yep."

I took the credit card from him and slipped it into my shirt pocket. He held onto the charge slip. He wanted to read Arkansas a little longer.

I said, "Well . . . " I shifted to the other foot. I said, "Time to get back on the road."

He said, "Texarkana."

I said, "Oh, your granddaddy. I see. Texarkana."

He said, "He's dead now."

I said "I'm sorry to hear it," and put my hand on the doorknob. I didn't need the receipt slip. And yet when I tried to leave, I couldn't. I looked at the boy, whose name might not have been

Jimmy Fish at all. He seemed even younger than before. My patriotism was gone, it seemed silly now. I felt very calm, and I began to see this boy in a way I had not been able to see before. He looked human to me for the first time. I thought maybe it was not just freaks I saw as less than human. Maybe it was everybody.

He said, "He died last weekend."

For some reason I had thought his grandfather had been dead much longer. I didn't answer right away. I said, "Just this last weekend."

This time he didn't answer.

I said, "Were you able to get over for the funeral?"

He said, "They didn't have a funeral."

I didn't know what to say. His grandfather had been left unburied for a full week.

The boy said, "His house burned down on him. Mama's still hunting bones." He handed me my receipt. He said, "Mama said no use burying him till we've got the whole thing."

I let a second or two pass. I said, "What's your granddaddy's name, Jimmy?" I wasn't reading his shirt. I said, "What did people call your granddaddy?"

He said, "Ellis."

I said, "Nice talking to you," and walked back out to the van.

Floyd was sitting in the shotgun seat ready to go. Winston was still in place in his chair.

I remembered something about my Grandmama Sugar. In the last two weeks of her life, she believed a band of Mexican midgets, with sombreros and ammunition belts, was camped in her bedroom. She thought they were playing cards and gambling at the foot of her bed at night. The day before she died she called me to her bed. She said, "They're not really there, Sugar. Don't pay any more attention to them than you have to."

I said, "All right, Sugar."

She said, "Muldrow was my youngest brother. You never knew him. He got a brain tumor and went blind and couldn't see anything but the inside of farm implement companies."

I said, "All right, Sugar, you rest now."

She said, "It's the same with these midget banditoes. They're not here either. No more than Muldrow's tractors and disks and haymows."

I said, "You rest."

She said, "Nothing is real." She said, "Nothing you see is ever really there."

I said, "All right."

She pointed to the Mexicans playing cards. Her voice was tolerant and loving. She said, "They're cute little buggers, but you can't understand a blessed word they say."

I got in the driver's seat. I said, "Winston, this is a long drive."

Winston said, "We're almost there."

I looked over at Floyd. The eclipse had passed. I could see him now, quite clearly. I said, "Floyd, how about you driving for a while."

Winston said, "I want you to drive, Sugar. You're a much better driver than Floyd."

I started up the engine.

Floyd got out and walked around to my side anyway. He stood outside the window.

I said, "It's okay, Floyd, I'll drive."

He said, "You start letting a cripple push you around, you're going to have a problem."

I looked out of the car at Jimmy Fish, where he stood in the fluorescent glare. I had never seen such a picture of loneliness.

Winston said, "Sugar, you start letting a cripple *and* a man as ugly as Floyd push you around, you've got a bigger problem."

They were right. It was time. I let Floyd slip behind the wheel and we pulled out. I wished we could take Jimmy Fish with us. I know he wanted to go. But there was no way it could be done. Just no way.

Sugar Mecklin was not right about one thing though, my grandmama. People *are* really there, every one of them. They definitely are. I swear, these are strange times we are living in.

WELCOME
TO THE
ARROW-CATCHER
FAIR

The usual long banner with red lettering had been strung from tree to tree on the pasture's edge: WELCOME TO THE ARROW-CATCHER FAIR. The Indian was shooting arrows, first from a small straight bow of hardwood, then from stronger, surer bows, and the Arrow Catcher was catching them. A crowd of spectators had gathered, but not so large a crowd as would congregate later.

Miss Golden Rondelle, the Arrow Catcher's sister, cursed softly the two of them. "You low-lifed fugitive from the Indian Removal Bill, Redboy, if you shoot one more arrow at that sweet child, gotdoggit, I'll . . . " And, still softly, "Arrow Catcher, I swear before the tomb of Tishomingo I wish I'd never paid for your shock therapy, you dried up little schizophrenic fart, you . . . " There were a few snickers from the nearest spectators, but not many. Her voice was soft, and this was a familiar curse, one that had lasted three years longer than three-quarters of a century, a curse spanning all those years since, in a wooded glen of wild pecan and tupelo and sweet gum, a five-year-old child at the turning of the century caught his first arrow and became the Arrow Catcher. Of the three the Arrow Catcher was youngest, the baby: he was eighty-three.

The fairgrounds covered a five-acre tract of flat but various ground, the well-mown bank of Roebuck Lake. Chickasaws in dugouts once floated upon these cypress-darkened waters past the single white-man's cabin and, pointing, named the spot in their own tongue, *biccauhgli*, a word that once meant perhaps "home in the woods" and later became the name of the town standing upon this site, Big Ugly, Mississippi.

There were camp tables and card tables and sawhorses laid with clean boards and covered with white tablecloths. Women set out hot casseroles and bowls of steaming vegetables and platters of sliced meats and fruit. There were Methodist folding chairs and Baptist coffee urns; there were plastic dispensers of iced tea and Kool Aid; there were stacks of paper plates and boxes of plastic forks. There was a bluegrass band from Memphis, and the community's Bicentennial flag was flying. Charles Kuralt was rumored to be in town.

There were bows and arrows everywhere, straight bows, recurved bows, hardwoods, fiberglass, laminations, longbows of yew, flat bows of lemonwood, steel bows with metal sights, stabilized bows, twins, monos, balls, and outriggers. There were all manner of archers, young and old, blind and sighted, crippled and crazy, those in uniforms and those near naked, Robin Hoods and college girls, snapshooters and practitioners of Zen, wheelchair archers and power archers, all of them in teams of two, an archer and a catcher, and in each team at least one who was willing to kill for the right to enter this competition and at least one willing to be killed for that right.

Or so most of them probably told themselves, though it was not true. Competition in the Arrow-Catcher Fair required rubber-tipped blunts, and while an arrow from a strong bow could knock a man down, injuries were rare. Most "misses" never touched the catcher, since a proper catch required at least a partial turning of the body, and arrow burns on the palms and fingers were the most common injury. Resin helped prevent blisters. The Arrow-Catcher Fair was, all agreed, no threat to the health of Mississippians; the true threat, according to local wags, was the annual Snuff-Dipping Convention in Grenada.

The first elimination trials were over. Last year's champion had been put away early, an arrow catcher of about sixty-five and his archer grandson. A youthful team from Montana made the first and second cuts and was as impressive as the rumors that preceded it here. There were other hopefuls as well, including a number of local teams.

The crowds grew larger, most of their number only spectators. Couples and families gathered on the grounds, a sweet hint of marijuana smoke hung in the air. Here a young mother dangled a careless foot in the cool lake's edge; there clustered a family beneath a spreading cottonwood. The women's competition was already finished; mixed team competition was in its last round. Charles Kuralt's CBS van had been spotted for certain, and—so another rumor had it—the governor of the state was on the grounds again this year.

The Montana team continued to practice, the archer standing at some forty yards' distance from his catcher. The archer drew and the arrow was gone. The catcher did not watch the arrow because he could not, he watched only a furrow in the atmosphere where he knew it flew. He did not feel his body turn left at thirty degrees because now the turning was reflexive, he did not know how he knew to make his sudden move toward the colored density that was the arrow because that too was reflex, he did not know how he plucked the arrow from the air and held it vibrating in his astonished hand. There was a small, desultory round of applause from the group that happened to be standing nearby. The Montana catcher tossed the arrow aside and waited for the next.

The scene was repeated many times throughout the little fair-grounds, archers and catchers performing for each other. But it was not these moments of practice or even the more tense moments of competition that were the true center of the day. The center was the blood and flesh of the three ancients who were the originals of this celebration, Redboy, Arrow Catcher, and Miss Golden, launching and catching and cursing, the first three human hearts to have quickened when the first wobbly arrow flew, a sharpened stick merely, almost fourscore years before from the Indian's homemade bow.

Golden's brother lost his real name at the age of five when he became the Arrow Catcher, and though Golden remembered her brother's birth that summer long ago on the mosquito-loud sleeping porch of their home, where her schizophrenic helpless mother lay upon a mattress stuffed with the down of fowls killed and plucked by Golden herself and beneath a clean comforter stitched with muscadines by Golden's grandmother during the Mexican War, she was not certain she remembered her brother's name. It might have been Gilbert. He had been the Arrow Catcher too long to remember.

She remembered her father as a quiet, gentle ghost who long ago slipped away from her mother's bedside and madness and was forgotten, who left before Arrow Catcher was born, and she remembered her mother only in bed, usually crying. Her memories survived from a time when the railroad came to Big Ugly. Her mother, beautiful and schizophrenic for many years before Mississippi even had a name for the problem, lay abed and wept and believed from the year 1894 until the day of her death that she herself was the train for which tracks were being laid near their home. "Chuffa-chuffa," that sick woman called during hard labor. "Chooooo choooooo," she had cried in childbirth. She believed also that in the large old drafty house in which she lay there were narrow-gauge rails on which in time of emergency she might fit her wheels and escape calamity, fire for example, or flood, both of which she expected almost daily. As a girl Golden sought and sought the tracks that her mother supposed lay upon their floors and never found them. For this folly she hated her mother. "Clickety-clack, clickety-clack," the poor woman said, considering her escape. Golden hid in a cedar wardrobe and wished she understood. "Clickety-clack, clickety-clack."

Golden hated the railroad, the real one, the felling of the trees, and the raising of great blackened timbers from which bark had been hacked for depot shingles, the timbers that would become the columns for the trestle across Roebuck, the iron and the hammers that made and laid the rails, the section gangs of bare-chested men, white and black, the oak that became the crossties and the rock that became the ballast, where, in the clash and clatter and clutter and enormity of its building, her mother's mind would steal quietly out of town and never be heard from again and in which her brother would catch his first arrow and become the Arrow Catcher.

It was in one of the years of the railroad's construction that Golden would first curse the Indian. "Listen to me, you no-count redskin," the child-woman would say, cursing above the trundle and thunder of construction, the clink of steel upon steel chiming in her brain as the rails went down, the first arrow from the first little willow bow already in flight as she spoke, and yet hardly an arrow at all, a sharpened branch of wild pecan in wobbly career toward the little white boy's bare frail breast, "if one of those pecan arrows hits my little brother, son," she would say on that morning of a leafy-warm mid-June when the Mississippi Delta air was already dense and heavy and sweet with humidity and honeysuckle, "you won't be able to trade your greasy scalp and nappy ass together for a handful of strung beads, so gotdoggit, Redboy, just be careful."

The five-year-old boy, her brother, already at so early an age beginning to withdraw like his mother into a strange quiet netherworld into which no one else, except perhaps the Indian, successfully entered, picked the arrow from the air like a bursting-ripe wild plum from a laden tree, and became in that moment the Arrow Catcher.

The red boy, older than the others but no one knew how old except that he was old enough to smell worse than the white children and most of the black ones, fitted another crude barreled shaft of pecan onto his bowstring and loosed a second shot.

Golden Rondelle cursed him again. "You useless low-class wild

Indian salvage bastard," she cried, "shame on your shameful red ass shooting sticks at that sweet little child, you are shameful and useless as tits on a boar hog shooting arrows at that child."

The quiet small hand of the Arrow Catcher collected the second speeding shaft from the air as easily as he might a fat late-summer firefly lazy with August.

The Indian child, handing his bow and a little clutch of arrows to Golden Rondelle, unhitched and took down his tattered filthy breeches to urinate into the lespedeza. "Hold my quiver, Goldie," he said. "I got to dreen my lizard."

Redboy no longer stank, and his clothes were neither tattered nor dirty. Today at the Arrow Catcher Fair he was a quiet ancient little man, almost black and no more than five-feet-four-inches tall, the tight mahogany of his skin rendering his face almost invisible in contrast to the brilliance of his false teeth. He wore a carefully tailored sport jacket of a fashionable cut, deep burgundy in color. The lenses of his sunglasses were also shaded burgundy. In his hands he held his best bow, a recurved composite with an ebony grip and a fifty-five-pound draw weight. A leather ground quiver of new arrows was stuck by its spike into the earth nearby.

"Arrow Catcher," said Golden Rondelle, trying again to remember whether they had named the child Gilbert and remembering only the down mattress and the unbleached muslin sheets and the comforter and remembering also the perfect little child, her brother, who had issued from her mother's body as Golden brought forth sweet artesian water drawn up from the cistern in a zinc bucket, remembering also the midwife, whom Golden called the granny-woman, the near-blind black woman who made the delivery, and remembering the clean glass jar of afterbirth and the placenta, which frightened her because she did not know what it was, and the strong white thread that cut the fleshy cord from her brother's body, "that renegade is going to shoot a hole through you one of these days big enough for a hen turkey to jump through and where please tell me will you be then?

Dead is where, so don't bother to make reply. I don't want to know."

"Hush up now, Miss Sister," the Arrow Catcher said, or might have said if he still spoke, as he had not for sixty-five years, but saying as much to Golden in his unspeaking as other men said with a million words, speaking perhaps through his beatific smile. "Hush now, Miss Sister, it's all right."

"Gotdoggit, Arrow Catcher," she said, "you were blessed from birth with the lowest blood pressure on the planet Earth and not enough sense to crap in a hole."

"Step back, Goldie," the Indian said, polite as always. "You don't want to give the boy reservations."

"Don't you get ironical with me, Redboy," she said, "because I have no reservations whatsoever about turning your hide into a Chickasaw hook rug and selling it in Oklahoma. And don't shoot another arrow at that white boy until I say so, do you understand me, or I'll make you think the Trail of Tears was the Amtrak Special to Miami. Gotdog. I can't stand an aboriginal."

The Indian chose an arrow from the ground quiver and inspected its fletching. Real feathers, four of them, and thick enough to slow the arrow drastically upon its leaving the bow. He liked to give the Arrow Catcher a few of these first, once he had started using the heavy bow. The sleek shafts with three narrow strips of plastic fletching would come later. Then he would alternate a few, some slow arrows among the swiftest. Therein lay the Arrow Catcher's true genius and mastery of time and space and the bodily organs. There was the reason the competition halted when the Arrow Catcher began work, and there was the reason the Arrow Catcher and the Indian were never a part of the competition and were never expected to be. Therein lay the artistry to which young men whose aspirations lay in the field of arrow catching aspired. He held the shaft lovingly in his hand, turning it. The blade—and this also was a difference between the Arrow Catcher and the rest—the blade that the Indian held and that the Arrow Catcher would catch was a bodkin, a triple-edged hunter's blade, solid sharp steel.

"Don't you do it, Redboy, don't you even think about it. Don't lay one more arrow on that string."

"Aw Goldie, come on now, hell," the Indian said, "give the boy time to think."

"Move back, Miss Sister," the Arrow Catcher might have said, though there was no sound, "move back, please'm."

"If you shoot that arrow, Redboy . . ."

The arrow was already gone. The bow from whose string the arrow flew was a precision instrument, a slender core of cedar laminated with fiber glass, and the arrow was not hardwood but a twenty-eight-inch tube of aluminum, a flu-flu arrow with three red fat turkey feathers and a yellow cock feather, an ariel hunting shaft, slow but with this bow faster than anything he had yet shot today. The arrow was in flight as the curse organized itself in Golden Rondelle's brain and upon her lips.

" . . . I'll fix you so . . ."

In near-invisible flight the arrow traveled the thirty brief yards that it would travel between its anchor point at the Indian's chin and its destination in the Arrow Catcher's hand or heart, the thick fletching bustling and ruffling against the air like a small covey of quail rising from sorghum . . .

" . . . your scalp won't sell for low-grade dog food . . ."

. . . not even quite visible, the shaft of aluminum, merely a disturbance of the atmosphere, not only to Golden Rondelle but to her brother the Arrow Catcher, who both saw and did not see, heard and did not hear the flurry and bustle and rush and flutter of tumultuous gossiping feathers, and yet not invisible quite, something there in the sun, metallic and swift and formless, a thickening . . .

" . . . I'll sell your scalp to a chiropractor with Ohio license plates . . ."

. . . and the Arrow Catcher, now as she watched him, seeing and not seeing, hearing for the first time distinctly the shaft bearing, preening down upon him, turned, only slightly, to his left, dropping his shoulder, the left shoulder, ever so slightly, and grasped in a perfect marriage of firmness and gentleness, as one lifts a warm speckled egg from beneath an old hen, in the smallest portion of a dangerous second, the hurtling aluminum streak. It was no longer the whispering whistling lustering mystery it had been one second earlier in the air. It was a quick momentary hum and drone upon his hand's flesh and in his ear and then nothing, a shaft of aluminum, a bodkin, four bright feathers. He tossed the arrow aside.

Golden was finished. Not all of the curse that passed through her mind was ever actually formed upon her tongue; there had been no time. The curse faltered and sputtered to a halt, stopped. Her little brother was safe.

"Let's go grab us a bite of that chicken and potato salad," said the Indian.

"I'm not eating fried chicken with an aboriginal, I can guarantee you that, Little Beaver," said Golden Rondelle.

They stopped now and ate without speaking. The crowd around them began to disperse. On the public address there was an announcement for qualifiers in the late rounds and then another announcement concerning novelty events.

The Arrow Catcher and the Indian sat facing different directions, eating little, and taking no coffee or tea, no stimulants. They rested and said nothing. Miss Golden sat apart from them, as she always did when the Indian was near, but in a position to see them both. She ate two helpings of bean salad with red onions.

The final arrows of the competition were shot and caught, the young Montana team progressing through the final round but losing, as expected, to an experienced pair of brothers from Bellafontaine. The bluegrass group was better than last year's, an energetic combination of banjos and harmonicas and guitars and a very tall young man with a washboard of elaborate design. *Bisquick* was the name printed on the drums.

Later the lieutenant governor was introduced from the bandstand and was helped up to the microphone. He was received with polite applause, and when the microphone and speakers stopped squealing he began his annual address, "Welcome, friends, welcome to the Arrow-Catcher Fair." As it became clear to the audience that the band was taking a break, there was a good deal of milling around and moving away from the platform to other parts of the grounds.

Still, some remained, and there was something about the speech that caught the ear of Miss Golden Rondelle. At first she could not hear well, so she turned and stood up, moving away from the Indian and the Arrow Catcher toward the speaker. She dropped the rest of the bean salad into the trash barrel. A few others had begun to listen as well, more than a few, a great many, though they had not intended to listen. The crowd moved back to the places where they had stood or sat for Bisquick and could not believe what they were seeing and hearing. The lieutenant governor was drunk and, whatever his subject, he was warming to it quickly. Charles Kuralt and CBS were filming and taping.

The lieutenant governor pointed across the fairgrounds at the raised flag of the Bicentennial. He spoke of the people of this great and solemn state—sovereign state, he had meant to say, correcting himself, then reneging on the correction and saying solemn again and again.

Miss Golden was at last close enough to hear, and now the noises of the crowd were quieting rapidly. The lieutenant governor had found his proper distance from the microphone and his voice rocked the Arrow-Catcher Fair like a calliope. Many were listening now, and others were on their way. The speech continued, wildly, the lieutenant governor borrowing freely from the Sermon on the Mount and Lincoln's Gettysburg Address and anything else that came to mind. "Hernando by-God de Soto," she heard him say. "Hernando buggering de Soto," he was saying, "great spic founder of this solemn state . . . " This was not the first time the lieutenant governor had embarrassed the state, but it was the first time on national television, and, as everyone must correctly have supposed, it would be the last time he would embarrass anyone ever again, for could there be any doubt that the governor would have him executed?

" . . . led a band of eccentric white men through this stinking buckshot and gumbo shithole that tries to pass for the real world and began," he said, "by mating with the abominable Chickasaw and Choctaw to people our solemn shores with lunatics, made these alluvial fields and pastures and piney woods and swamps and bearcats and all our abominations of geography America's first and last rich stronghold of lunacy and feeblemindedness and dwarfism in a proud and unhappy land . . . "

The crowd was dumbstruck. They were both moved to laughter and unable to laugh. They were silent and horrified; they were mass silence masking hysteria. Every man and woman among them was scandalized and stood in dread of some unnamed impending doom about to fall like acid rain upon the state and this pasture. Those who liked the lieutenant governor and those who despised him were equally scandalized and horrified, those who voted for him and those who had threatened him with homicide. It was a dark day for the Arrow-Catcher Fair.

" . . . proud of our individualism in Mississippi," he was saying, "individually, man for man, woman for woman, child for child, the most individually obscene and corrupt populace and geography, save only Los Angeles and Gary, Indiana, in an entire obscene civilization . . . "

To all who watched and listened, it was finally clear: this was no ordinary drunken scene at a fair. This was no ordinary exhibition of a failed man and a ruined rummy politician. This was the ugly deliberate song of a mortally wounded political swan, a deliberate humiliation of the governor and of the entire state. "This is Charles Kuralt" was the phrase that in this crowd every mind's ear heard upon every mind's evening news, "on the road. Welcome to the Arrow-Catcher Fair." Someone rushed from the crowd to find out whether the governor had yet left the fairgrounds. A large red-haired, red-faced man stood reduced to tears, begging Charles Kuralt please to stop the cameras.

" . . . proud," the lieutenant governor was saying, "of our individualism, proud of our pain, we are proud of our neurotic romanticism and our feelings of inferiority, proud of our pathetic apologies and of our pathetic failures to apologize, proud of the bloody stains of our guilt, we are proud of our psychotic rage never to question or wonder and always to justify and create . . . "

A shout came from the crowd. The governor was on his way, someone cried. Make way for the governor. There was a sudden release of the silent storm inside the crowd, a partial release anyway, a flurry of whispers and uncertain movement and coughing. "Come on down, Lee," an older man at the foot of the platform said to the speaker, "come on down, man, that's enough, god-amighty." But the lieutenant governor did not stop.

" . . . proud," he said again, pointing again irrationally at the flag and again no less careless of historical accuracy, "to have become inhabitants of this blessed land of perversity, founded by an insane Spaniard in his insane and successful discovery of that mightiest of insane rivers, insane father of insane waters, potent puissant pregnant pointless pissant stream! That very snakish flood in which God's own unholy self of the Holy Ghost resides, yea verily I say unto you, even unto this day in the form of an alligator gar, molded from the Mississippi clay by God's own mighty hand upon Christ's eternal wheel in prescient anticipation of our present governor's mind and soul and face, I have a dream, brothers and sisters, I have a dream . . . "

Two state troopers in uniform mounted the bandstand and tried to lead him gently away. He would not be led. Both troopers, trying not to face the whirring cameras, were embarrassed literally to tears. They tugged at him and he would not move. There was a scuffle, a brief struggle, which the lieutenant governor won because the troopers were unsure what to do, how much force to use. "Turn off the camera, Mr. Kuralt, please Jesus just turn it off," one of the troopers begged, directly into the microphone, but the film kept rolling.

Unnoticed, across the pasture, the Indian and the Arrow Catcher had begun work again, shooting arrows and catching them. Golden Rondelle, in these first stirrings of a recognition of the futility of her own bitterness, had forgotten to watch out for her brother. She was not there to curse them.

" . . . I have a dream," said the lieutenant governor, kicking at those who would restrain him, "of the scaly, snouted gar–God and life–giver and life–destroyer of all Mississippians submerged in the bloody rivers of our lands and hearts . . . " He held the microphone in a passionate triumphant death–grip, the state troopers tugging hopelessly at his shirt. The governor of the state, a handsome man in a white Prince Albert suit, mounted the platform, grappling with the lieutenant governor for the microphone, but in the confusion could not wrest it from him. One of the troopers, suddenly feeling sorry for the lieutenant governor, began to fight on his side. Fists flew, none of them yet touching the lieutenant governor.

" . . . eternal sustainer of our inherited alluvial madness and more green–headed mallard drakes in the rice brakes than you can shake a shitty stick at, hand me up that Co–Cola bottle, sonny, I got to dreench my weasle . . . "

His words were becoming incoherent now and crazy and something in them and behind them—it was the distant but very real sound of a diesel freight that Golden did not know yet that she heard—made her remember what she had forgotten, the Indian and her little brother.

Frantic, she looked behind her, far across the astonished flood of faces, and saw the two of them. "Arrow Catcher!" she screamed, already pushing through the crowd. "Redboy!" People stepped aside for her, she bumped against them roughly, making her way. "Redboy, don't do it! Arrow Catcher! This is the hour of your death!"

On the bandstand there was a second, more violent struggle, and this time the speaker was subdued. He fell to the platform, kicking and biting and cursing. The microphone crashed to the earth, the amplifier screaming, the lieutenant governor grabbing for it and pulling it to him where he lay. Several men fell on top of the downed lieutenant governor, the two troopers and the governor among them, scuffling and scratching and punching. "Goddamn this very Delta earth beneath our feet," boomed the calliope voice of the amplifiers, "goddamn these spreading trees, goddamn these matchless Mississippi blue skies." These were the last words audible in the struggle.

The train was approaching the trestle. Golden's only thought was of death; she could not say why.

"It is the hour of your death, dear Lincoln," she cried to her brother. "Don't release the arrow, Redboy, or Lincoln will die!" So that was the child-man's name, she thought, her brother's name. Lincoln, not Gilbert. She had remembered. It seemed impossible that she should ever have forgotten.

She shoved and jostled and bumped and pushed. The crowd opened for her but slowly. Lincoln had caught two arrows since she started making her way toward him. At last she broke through the unsteady crust of the crowd's edge and began running, as fast as she could, old woman with the yellow hoot and rumble of the diesel in her ears, across the pasture, straight for her brother. She was still screaming. Lincoln had caught another arrow.

There was time somehow to wonder at the coincidence of the lieutenant governor's insane speech and the approach of the train to the trestle. She wondered whether it was really a coincidence at all that these two things should happen just as she remembered her brother's name. She believed rather that on this instant she had suddenly become old enough and wise enough and bitter enough to swim beyond her lost childhood and bitterness and to take all the earth's available phenomena, natural, mechanical, and political, and shape them into meaning. The speech from the platform had made her old enough; the approach of the freight translated the lieutenant governor's voice to the voice of memory. She ran toward her brother, screaming. She reached him, calling his name, Lincoln Lincoln Lincoln. She touched him.

As she did, as her hand felt the soft fabric of his shirt and felt through the fabric the tense little muscles of her brother's shoulder, she thought, Uh-oh. She thought, I shouldn't have done this. Redboy has not seen me, he sees nothing but his target. He hears nothing. An arrow will be leaving his bow soon, and my hand on this little shoulder may distract, may prevent my brother from catching it. She wondered if the arrow would hit her brother, or if it would hit herself. It could scarcely be hoped to miss both of them. Or could it? He had never missed before, not once in decades. But he had never been touched upon the shoulder while trying. Oh dear, oh shit.

Too late the Indian saw Golden Rondelle move into the tunnel of his pinpoint-focused vision, the narrow squinty line of sight that was the concentrated entirety of his attention. Too late he saw that the bowstring was no longer in his fingertips, that the arrow was already inexorably launched.

The arrow carried a broadhead, a razor-sharp hunting blade of triangular shape, and the fletching was sleek swift plastic. She thought, though there was no time for thought, that the sound of the train, both the remembered steam engine in her mind and the yellow diesel not forty yards away on the trestle, was the sound of her mother's voice: "Chuffa-chuffa," during labor. "Choooooo choooooo," during birth. "Clickety-clack," in her imagined escape from fire and flood and probably from everything else that this handkerchief-sized spot of earth had meant to her.

As the train approached the trestle, Golden thought that not far from here where we stand waiting upon death or salvation there are children waiting. If children were today the same as they had been so many years ago, they were hiding in the great ditch bordering the tracks, waiting in lespedeza and Johnson grass and wild chinaberries, children black and white and even red, boys and girls, waiting for the train to slow almost to stopping before it crossed the Roebuck trestle. There were children, she thought, at this moment waiting until the last possible second to rush from their hiding to grab the cold ladder of a boxcar, to pull themselves shrieking and squealing and swinging aboard. These children would, as Golden and Redboy and Lincoln had done, ride the train across the trestle triumphant and then, like the lieutenant governor, jump suicidal to safety before the train took speed again on the other side.

The voice of the train was the voice of her mother naming rivers, as sometimes for hours she would do, the rivers and tributaries of Mississippi, most of them with Chickasaw and Choctaw names, the rivers she would cross when all the trestles were built and she would be allowed to roll free at last from the bed of her affliction and confusion and from the geography that had confused her. "Coldwater," the woman-train would begin, slowly, "Yazoo," still slowly, "Yazoo, Yocona," heaving, straining for even the smallest increase of speed, "Yocona, Skuna, Bogue, Hickahala," faster now, faster and faster, sobbing deeply and more deeply, "Hickahala, Hickahala, Yalobusha Yalobusha Tallahatchie Tallahatchie whoooooo whooooooo!" faster and faster, into the final register, crossing at full tilt the mighty river at Greenville, not even bothering to slow down for the trestle, "Tallahatchie Tallahatchie Mississippi Mississippi Mississippi, whooooo whooooooo!" headed west, westward westward forever and away.

And if there are children there today, she thought, waiting in their secret ditch for the train, this yellow diesel, was there not also in the reeds among them a little girl, as once she had been, whose mother was too sick ever to tell her she was pretty? Was there in the reedy ditch or on the boxcar's rusty ladder one who, like Golden Rondelle, reared her mother and was not reared by her? who reared her brother and forgot her father and forgot her brother's name? and before that a child who watched, still holding the zinc bucket so heavy with sweet water that it cut into her little palm, her brother's painful emergence like that of a train from a tunnel unimaginably deep and dangerous? a child whom first she would protect as a man-child and then, as he joined his mother, and somehow also the Indian, in a netherworld in which he might escape his original emergence, protect him as a child-man? Was there a child in the blackberry vines this moment as the arrow flew who found for so many years no source from which to draw either strength or sweetness and so drew it from within herself, from the deep cistern of heart behind the sweet face which no mother ever told her was beautiful, though then it was and even as the arrow continued in its flight remained so, drawing from this deep but finite source, unreplenished and unreplenishable, until she became almost as crazy as her mother and brother? And yet a child who, after so long, did love her brother and loved, at least in this insane moment, the strange memory of her strange sick mother and felt, painfully, an emotion for the Indian that she had carried inside her for so long and which even now in its sweetness she found impossible to give a name, knowing, however, something of that emotion because for so many years she had seen it shared between Lincoln and the Indian in their dangerous necessary game of habitual love made possible by death's terrible, sweet omnipresence.

Golden watched, though there was no time to watch, and saw, though even the slow arrows were invisible, the loosed arrow as it left its place upon the bow and string, this fastest and most dangerous of arrows. It seemed to bend upon the bow, first right then left, then to straighten itself in flight. Oh, this swift arrow was a deadly arrow and, as it slammed shut the distance between the archer and the catcher and as her fingers' grip tightened upon her brother's shoulder, she remembered that the Indian's name was Gilbert. So, she thought, that was why she had been mixed up. So Gilbert is the Indian's name, she thought. Hmm. Well, it's not a bad name, not at all. It's a nice name. But it's a damn strange name for an Indian.

ABOUT THE AUTHOR

Lewis Nordan, a native of Itta Bena, Mississippi, is assistant professor of creative writing at the University of Pittsburgh. His stories have appeared in the *Greensboro Review, Harpers, Redbook,* and the *Southern Review.* He won the John Gould Fletcher award for fiction in 1977. His previous collection of short stories, *The All-Girl Football Team,* is also available in Vintage Contemporaries.

VINTAGE
CONTEMPORARIES

___	**Love Always** by Ann Beattie	$5.95	394-74418-7
___	**First Love and Other Sorrows** by Harold Brodkey	$7.95	679-72075-8
___	**The Debut** by Anita Brookner	$5.95	394-72856-4
___	**Cathedral** by Raymond Carver	$6.95	679-72369-2
___	**Fires** by Raymond Carver	$7.95	679-72239-4
___	**What We Talk About When We Talk About Love** by Raymond Carver	$5.95	679-72305-6
___	**Where I'm Calling From** by Raymond Carver	$8.95	679-72231-9
___	**Bop** by Maxine Chernoff	$5.95	394-75522-7
___	**I Look Divine** by Christopher Coe	$5.95	394-75995-8
___	**Dancing Bear** by James Crumley	$6.95	394-72576-X
___	**The Last Good Kiss** by James Crumley	$6.95	394-75989-3
___	**One to Count Cadence** by James Crumley	$5.95	394-73559-5
___	**The Wrong Case** by James Crumley	$5.95	394-73558-7
___	**The Last Election** by Pete Davies	$6.95	394-74702-X
___	**Great Jones Street** by Don DeLillo	$7.95	679-72303-X
___	**The Names** by Don DeLillo	$7.95	679-72295-5
___	**Players** by Don DeLillo	$6.95	679-72293-9
___	**Ratner's Star** by Don DeLillo	$8.95	679-72292-0
___	**Running Dog** by Don DeLillo	$6.95	679-72294-7
___	**A Narrow Time** by Michael Downing	$6.95	394-75568-5
___	**The Commitments** by Roddy Doyle	$6.95	679-72174-6
___	**From Rockaway** by Jill Eisenstadt	$6.95	394-75761-0
___	**Platitudes** by Trey Ellis	$6.95	394-75439-5
___	**Days Between Stations** by Steve Erickson	$6.95	394-74685-6
___	**Rubicon Beach** by Steve Erickson	$6.95	394-75513-8
___	**A Fan's Notes** by Frederick Exley	$7.95	679-72076-6
___	**Pages from a Cold Island** by Frederick Exley	$6.95	394-75977-X
___	**A Piece of My Heart** by Richard Ford	$6.95	394-72914-5
___	**Rock Springs** by Richard Ford	$6.95	394-75700-9
___	**The Sportswriter** by Richard Ford	$6.95	394-74325-3
___	**The Ultimate Good Luck** by Richard Ford	$5.95	394-75089-6
___	**Bad Behavior** by Mary Gaitskill	$6.95	679-72327-7
___	**Fat City** by Leonard Gardner	$6.95	394-74316-4
___	**Ellen Foster** by Kaye Gibbons	$5.95	394-75757-2
___	**Within Normal Limits** by Todd Grimson	$5.95	394-74617-1
___	**Airships** by Barry Hannah	$5.95	394-72913-7
___	**Dancing in the Dark** by Janet Hobhouse	$5.95	394-72588-3
___	**November** by Janet Hobhouse	$6.95	394-74665-1
___	**Saigon, Illinois** by Paul Hoover	$6.95	394-75849-8
___	**Angels** by Denis Johnson	$7.95	394-75987-7
___	**Fiskadoro** by Denis Johnson	$6.95	394-74367-9

VINTAGE
CONTEMPORARIES

___ **The Stars at Noon** by Denis Johnson	$5.95	394-75427-1
___ **Asa, as I Knew Him** by Susanna Kaysen	$4.95	394-74985-5
___ **Lulu Incognito** by Raymond Kennedy	$7.95	394-75641-X
___ **Steps** by Jerzy Kosinski	$5.95	394-75716-5
___ **A Handbook for Visitors From Outer Space** by Kathryn Kramer	$5.95	394-72989-7
___ **The Chosen Place, the Timeless People** by Paule Marshall	$6.95	394-72633-2
___ **A Recent Martyr** by Valerie Martin	$7.95	679-72158-4
___ **The Consolation of Nature and Other Stories** by Valerie Martin	$6.95	679-72159-2
___ **Suttree** by Cormac McCarthy	$6.95	394-74145-5
___ **California Bloodstock** by Terry McDonell	$7.95	679-72168-1
___ **The Bushwhacked Piano** by Thomas McGuane	$5.95	394-72642-1
___ **Nobody's Angel** by Thomas McGuane	$6.95	394-74738-0
___ **Something to Be Desired** by Thomas McGuane	$4.95	394-73156-5
___ **To Skin a Cat** by Thomas McGuane	$5.95	394-75521-9
___ **Bright Lights, Big City** by Jay McInerney	$5.95	394-72641-3
___ **Ransom** by Jay McInerney	$5.95	394-74118-8
___ **Story of My Life** by Jay McInerney	$5.95	679-72257-2
___ **Mama Day** by Gloria Naylor	$7.95	679-72181-9
___ **The All-Girl Football Team** by Lewis Nordan	$5.95	394-75701-7
___ **Welcome to the Arrow-Catcher Fair** by Lewis Nordan	$6.95	679-72164-9
___ **River Dogs** by Robert Olmstead	$6.95	394-74684-8
___ **Soft Water** by Robert Olmstead	$6.95	394-75752-1
___ **Family Resemblances** by Lowry Pei	$6.95	394-75528-6
___ **Norwood** by Charles Portis	$5.95	394-72931-5
___ **Clea & Zeus Divorce** by Emily Prager	$6.95	394-75591-X
___ **A Visit From the Footbinder** by Emily Prager	$6.95	394-75592-8
___ **Mohawk** by Richard Russo	$6.95	394-74409-8
___ **Anywhere But Here** by Mona Simpson	$6.95	394-75559-6
___ **Carnival for the Gods** by Gladys Swan	$6.95	394-74330-X
___ **The Player** by Michael Tolkin	$7.95	679-72254-8
___ **Myra Breckinridge and Myron** by Gore Vidal	$8.95	394-75444-1
___ **The Car Thief** by Theodore Weesner	$6.95	394-74097-1
___ **Breaking and Entering** by Joy Williams	$6.95	394-75773-4
___ **Taking Care** by Joy Williams	$5.95	394-72912-9
___ **The Easter Parade** by Richard Yates	$8.95	679-72230-0
___ **Eleven Kinds of Loneliness** by Richard Yates	$8.95	679-72221-1
___ **Revolutionary Road** by Richard Yates	$8.95	679-72191-6

Now at your bookstore or call toll-free to order: 1-800-638-6460
(credit cards only).